SWEENEY SIST

boots
and
bedlam

a novella

ASHLEY
FARLEY

For my patient and supportive husband

ONE

CARDBOARD BOXES, WORN from years of use, and large plastic storage bins packed with decorations littered every surface of Samantha Sweeney's sitting room as she sat against the wall next to an electrical outlet testing strands of white lights one by one. Sam had a standing appointment with her son, Jamie, for the Saturday after Thanksgiving to string the lights up on the outside of the house. She'd taken the day off from her family's seafood business with this purpose in mind, but he had disappeared right after lunch. And, after hauling the boxes and bins down from the attic, she lacked the energy to do it herself.

The back door in the kitchen creaked open. Seconds later Eli entered the room, stopping short when he saw her sitting on the floor in tattered jeans, a USC sweatshirt, and a baseball cap pulled low, hiding much of her face. "Don't take this the wrong way. I think you look hot in your work clothes. But I hope you're not planning to wear them out to dinner."

"Don't be ridiculous. Of course I'm not wearing this out

to dinner." She glanced at the clock on the mantel. "It's only five thirty. I thought you weren't coming until six. And why are you so dressed up?"

Dressed up for Eli meant his khaki pants were pressed and he wore the nicer of the three flannel shirts he owned—the plaid one from the men's store on Main Street that she'd given him for his birthday.

"Since when is it wrong for a man to want to look nice for his girl?" Holding out his hand to her, he pulled her to her feet. "We have a reservation. They'll hold it for us, but you'd better put it in gear."

"What reservation? I thought we were going to the Pelican's Roost for dinner?"

"Change of plans. I'm taking you somewhere special tonight. Go!" He smacked her on the rear. "Put on something pretty."

"Please tell me I don't have to wear a dress," she said, walking backward as she exited the room.

He let out a bark of laughter. "Since when do you own a dress?"

"Funny, ha-ha. I actually own two."

"A dress isn't necessary unless you just feel like wearing one. Which I'm sure you don't. Hurry." He shooed her out of the room. "We're gonna be late."

Sam went in the bathroom. She was turning on the shower when she heard the sportscaster announced the score of the Alabama-Auburn game on the TV in the other room.

Maybe I can convince him to stay home, order a pizza, and watch football. What man doesn't want to watch the college teams play their big rivals?

Wishful thinking. She stripped off her clothes and

stepped in the shower. She'd seen the determined set of his jaw. He had something up his sleeve.

Despite Eli's insistence that she hurry, she took extra time with her appearance, styling her short hair and applying a touch of makeup—a swipe of clear gloss to her rosy lips and a hint of blush to her pale cheeks. She slipped on her one pair of designer jeans and a white silky blouse that clung to her slight figure before tugging on her cowboy boots.

When she emerged from her bedroom twenty minutes later, Eli was waiting for her in the hallway. "Turn around and place your hands against the wall."

"Ooh . . . I like the sound of that. Are you planning to frisk me, Officer?"

"No, ma'am. I'm placing you under arrest." After a quick pat down, he covered her eyes with a blindfold. "You'll need this. It's cold outside." The familiar weight of her Barbour coat cocooned her body.

"I guess this means we can't stay home and watch football."

"No football tonight. Sorry." He spun her around and fastened something cold and hard, which she assumed were handcuffs, around her wrists.

"What exactly do you have in mind for me tonight, Lt. Marshall?"

"You'll have to wait and see." He scooped her off her feet and carried her outside to the car—her Jeep judging from the squeaky passenger door and the smell of mildew inside.

"Where are we going?" she asked when he set her down on the seat.

"Stop asking so many questions. You'll find out when we get there," he said, and slammed the door.

Sam kept track of the number of turns and the time in

between each one. When she felt a bump and the crunch of gravel beneath the wheels, she guesstimated they were on the waterfront somewhere close to her younger sister Faith's house. The Jeep rolled to a stop, the engine grew silent, and the driver's door opened and closed. Seconds later Eli was at her side, gripping her arm tight as she climbed out. He removed the handcuffs and untied the bandanna from her head. She rubbed her wrists and blinked her eyes until they adjusted to the scene in front of her.

Tiki torches lined the stone sidewalk leading to a low-slung house with coffee-colored hardy plank siding and black Bahamas-style hurricane shutters. Despite the Cape Cod-style dormer windows, Sam classified the bungalow as midcentury modern.

"Who lives here?" she asked.

"No one at the moment. It's on the market." Eli took her by the arm and guided her to the front stoop. "But if it meets your approval, I may make an offer."

A short entry hall led to a great room with stone fireplaces occupying the walls on both sides and a bank of windows and french doors in front of her. She assumed the doors opened onto a porch or deck although it was too dark outside to tell. Standing in the center of the room was her handsome son with his too-long dark hair curling up over the collar of his white button-down shirt.

"Welcome, folks. I'll be your server for the evening," Jamie said in a deep voice.

"Young man, what have you done with my son?" She ran her hand down his cheek. "You look like him, but your voice is much too deep and formal."

"Can I offer you a glass of sparkling wine?" Jamie

boots and bedlam

a novella

Also by Ashley Farley

presented a tray bearing two champagne flutes fizzing with sparkling wine. "It's nonalcoholic of course."

Sam removed a glass from the tray. "So this is where you've been all day. I've been waiting at home for you to help me with the lights."

"I'm sorry, Mom," he said in his normal voice. "Eli asked me to help him out. I couldn't very well tell him no."

Sam smiled, thinking that even though Jamie had grown up without a father, Eli had become a wonderful stand-in and had formed a relationship with Jamie that was more about friendship than parental authority.

"What is all this anyway?" Sam noticed the round table set for two with crystal and linens in front of one of the fireplaces. "Are we eating here?"

"We are." Eli took her by the hand. "Come with me, and I'll show you the kitchen and introduce you to the chefs."

Sam followed Eli into the adjoining room. Known in the Lowcountry as the connoisseur of seafood, her mother, Lovie Sweeney, was working side by side at the kitchen counter with Jamie's half sister, Annie.

Lovie looked up from her cutting board, her gnarled fingers wrapped around the black handle of a butcher knife. "I just love this kitchen, Samantha. If you don't buy this charming house, I might."

"I hate to tell you, Mom, but I'm not the potential buyer." Sam aimed her thumb at Eli. "He is."

"This house does have a certain masculine feel to it. Especially in here." Lovie waved her knife around.

Sam took in the handsomely appointed kitchen—the heavy millwork on the gray cabinets and the mahogany countertops.

Annie gestured at the Wolf range. "I can totally see Louis Tikaram cooking at that stove."

"Who is Louis Tikaram?" Sam asked.

Her mouth fell open. "Where have you been, Sam? He's one of the top up-and-coming chefs in the country."

Jamie rolled his eyes. "You just think he's hot."

"That too," she said, a smile spreading across her lips and reaching her eyes—the eyes that resembled Jamie's in shape, wide set and upturned, but not in color. Hers were nut brown, while his were as black as a stormy sky.

"Think of all the entertaining we can do in this kitchen." Eli stepped back from the counter where they were standing. "You can put at least three bar stools here. And seat six or seven more people over there." He pointed at the built-in banquette against the south wall where an attractive middle-aged woman with a silver bob sat typing away on her laptop.

"Sheila, this is Samantha Sweeney. Sam, meet Sheila Townsend, my realtor."

Sheila wiggled her fingers at Sam. "Don't mind me. The owners insisted I be here. Consider me invisible."

"I'm sure the owners are motivated to sell, but it was nice of them to let Eli host his dinner here nonetheless." Sam leaned across the counter to Annie and Lovie. "I'm sure these two will feed you. What's for dinner, by the way?"

"It's a surprise," Lovie said.

Sam eyed the gooey patty in Annie's hands. "Looks like crab cakes to me."

Annie's eyebrows reached her honey-colored hairline. "You should know by now that a crab cake is never just a crab cake when Lovie and I are in the kitchen."

"Go on now." Lovie pointed her knife at the door. "Leave us to our work."

Taking her by the hand, Eli led Sam back across the great room and into the master bedroom. "I'm not sure what to think about all these windows," she said, when she encountered yet another wall of glass. "The view must be incredible during the day, but right now, at night, I feel like a guppy in a fishbowl."

He rubbed the scruff on his chin as he considered the windows. "I know what you mean. Can't we throw up some curtains or something?"

"Plantation shutters or roll-down shades might work better."

"Wait until you see the bathroom." He gestured for her to follow him into the en suite bath.

She ran her fingers across the smooth countertop. "This marble must have cost someone a fortune." She ventured into the glass-enclosed walk-in shower. "And this shower is bigger than my garage. I would need a fire hose and a water tower full of Windex to clean it."

Eli pinned her against the wall and planted a trail of kisses on her neck. "Think how much fun we could have in here."

She pushed his head away. "Stop! My family is in the other room."

"I can't help myself," he said as he dove in for another nibble of her neck. "The cowboy boots drive me crazy. I want to see you wearing them naked."

She untangled herself from his embrace and straightened her clothes. "You better show me the rest of the house before you get carried away and embarrass yourself."

The tour of the small but adequate upstairs took less than five minutes. Jamie was waiting to refill their glasses when they returned to the great room. "Your appetizers will be ready soon." He punched in a series of commands on a control panel beside the doorway to the kitchen. The lights dimmed and jazz music began to play softly from the speakers in the ceiling. Jamie turned to face them. "Can I get anything else for you while you wait?"

"We're fine, honey, but thank you," Sam said. "You're doing a nice job as a waiter."

"I know what you're thinking, Mom, but don't worry. I'm not planning to drop out of college and become a waiter." He retreated to the kitchen, pulling the pocket door closed behind him.

"So, what do you think?" Eli asked, his arms spread wide.

"I have mixed emotions. But overall, I agree with Mom that it has a certain charm. How long has it been on the market?"

"For a while. There's a good chance they'll accept a low-ball offer."

"I can't believe the realtor let you do all this." She tossed her hands in the air, sending a stream of wine splashing to the floor.

Eli removed the bandanna from his back pocket and wiped up the spill. "Apparently the owners are desperate to sell."

"Did they move away?"

"No, they're from up north somewhere. They used this as a second home." He pocketed the bandanna.

"I can see why it might be hard to sell. It's not exactly user-friendly for a family with small children. There's no place for them to play except in here and the two bedrooms upstairs. A first-floor master would work for us, but I can't imagine being that far away from a baby or small child at night." Sam wandered around the room, exploring it from every angle. "I'm not creative enough to figure out how to use this space. It's one gigantic square that would need to serve multiple purposes."

"Sam, you have a sister who just happens to be an interior designer. We'll hire her. Jackie will know how to handle it."

Sam sipped her wine. "You keep referring to we, like you're planning on me moving in with you. Is that what you're thinking?"

"That's what I'm hoping." He set her champagne flute on the mantel above the fireplace and took her hands in his. "Before you get all worked up, just hear me out. I promised you last summer, when we got back together after our breakup, that I would refrain from using the *c* word. But you seem to have come to terms with your fear of commitment."

"That's because you haven't been pressuring me."

"Please, let me finish." He winked at her. "Yes, I'm hoping you'll move in here with me. As my wife. These past six months have been the best. At least for me. We can have the happily ever after, if you're willing to give us a chance. We can wait five years if that's what you want, but I'd rather you say yes right now so we can move on with our lives together. Whether that means in this cool bungalow with the sexy master bath or another house somewhere down the road, literally and figuratively."

She cocked her head, waiting for him to continue. When he remained silent, she said, "Am I allowed to speak yet?"

"By all means."

"My answer is yes."

His gray eyes brightened like shiny silver dollars. "You mean . . ."

She nodded her head vigorously. "Yes, I'll marry you."

"Wait a minute. I'm confused." He dropped her hands and raked his fingers through his thick dark hair. "I fully expected you to argue, or get mad and storm out, or—"

"Shh!" She held her finger to his lips. "It's my turn to talk. You're right. Things have been great between us, Eli. You are good for me. I couldn't love another person more than I love you. Until I started seeing you, I'd only been on a handful of dates since Jamie's father left me. I freaked out last summer, because I was confused, because it was all happening too fast for me. But I've learned a lot about myself since then. I know what I want. And more than anything, I want to be your wife."

He dug his hand in his pocket and pulled out a diamond engagement ring. "This was my grandmother's. I hope you like it." He slipped the ring on her finger.

She bit down on her quivering lip. "It's beautiful." She held her hand out, admiring the way the light bounced off the diamond solitaire. "How special that it belonged to your grandmother." She wrapped her arms around his neck and kissed him on the lips. "If you break my heart, Eli Marshall, you'll have to contend with my son."

"Funny, Jamie said that very thing to me when I asked his permission last week."

She drew back from him. "You actually asked my son for permission to marry me?"

"He would've been disappointed if I hadn't."

"You're right about that," she said, smiling. "What about Mom and Annie? Considering your elaborate scheme, I'm guessing they know you were planning to propose as well."

The pocket door slid open revealing three eager faces. "Of

course we knew about the proposal." With outstretched arms, Lovie crossed the room in three strides. "And it's a darn good thing you said yes. Or you would be answering to the three of us."

Lovie's body felt frail against Sam's, a reminder that her mother would turn eighty-four in January. She held Sam at arm's length while she studied her face. "Good for you, Sammie," she said, chucking her on the chin, like a coach to her Little League baseball player.

Jamie smacked Eli on the back. "And you're right. I would've been disappointed if you hadn't asked my permission."

"Let me see the ring!" Annie grabbed Sam's hand and brought it up close to her face. "It's so beautiful. I'm so happy for you." She threw herself into Sam's arms.

"Thank you, sweetheart," Sam said, removing a strand of Annie's hair from her mouth. "I'm glad you're sharing this special moment with us."

"Stand in front of the fire, and let me take your picture," Jamie ordered.

Eli dragged Sam over to the fireplace. "You can text it to our family, but don't you dare put it on social media," she said.

"Only on Facebook," Jamie said as he began to click the pics on his iPhone.

Once Jamie had gotten the shot he wanted, Eli pulled him aside. "Whatever you do, don't say anything about the house, especially on Facebook." He squeezed Jamie's shoulder. "We haven't decided whether to make an offer or not."

Jamie nodded. "Understood."

"Come on, you two." Lovie pointed Jamie and Annie toward the kitchen. "Let's give these lovebirds a minute alone while we put the finishing touches on dinner."

Eli waited for them to leave before seating Sam at the table in front of the fireplace. "Happy?" he asked as he pulled out the chair opposite her.

She bobbed her blonde head up and down. "Very."

"I will totally understand if you want to wait six months or a year before we get married. We can have a big traditional wedding or a small family wedding. I'm up for anything."

"I don't want to wait. I'd marry you right here, right now if I could." She leaned across the table to him. "How does a small family wedding on Christmas Eve sound?"

His eyebrows shot up. "Christmas Eve? That's only four weeks away. Why so soon? Are you worried you'll get cold feet and change your mind about marrying me?"

She lay her hand on his. "On the contrary. You know how I am. Patience is not one of my virtues. Once I make my mind up to do something, I want it done right away."

His lips curled into a smile, and the dimple she loved so much appeared on his cheek. "Okay then. Christmas Eve it is."

TWO

THE WEDDING BELLS ringtone, which Jamie had set on Sam's cell phone the previous evening, startled her out of a deep sleep early on Sunday morning. Struggling to sit up, she snatched the phone off the nightstand.

"Morning, beautiful," Eli said, his voice husky from sleep. "You didn't have a change of heart during the night about marrying me, did you?"

The sight of the diamond engagement ring on her hand summoned a smile to her lips. "We settled this last night, Eli. I can hardly wait to be your wife." She glanced at her alarm clock. "It's only eight o'clock. Why are you calling so early? Is something wrong?"

"What could possibly be wrong on a day like today? It's just that the realtor is harassing me about making an offer on the house."

She drew her knees up, tucking them under her chin. "But it's Sunday morning. Can't she wait? At least until after church."

"Apparently the owners are traveling out of the country this afternoon," Eli said. "They will be gone for a couple of weeks. If we want to make an offer, we need to do it today."

"I highly doubt that's true, Eli. Realtors are experts at manipulating their clients into making quick decisions."

"She's been more than fair with me, Sammie. Allowing me to use the house last night to propose to you was above and beyond her call of duty."

Sam smiled into the phone. "I agree. Your proposal was very thoughtful. It wins the prize for best proposals, in fact. At least in the Sweeney family. But that doesn't mean you should feel obligated to make an offer. Do you really like this house that much?"

"I do, but I sense you still have some reservations. I want you to walk through again during the day. I think you'll be more comfortable with making an offer once you see the view."

Sam peeled the covers back. "In that case, I'll meet you in thirty minutes."

❄

Eli was right. The bungalow was a remarkably different place in the daylight with the sun streaming in through the banks of windows that offered panoramic views of the waterfront. The inlet views struck her as a singular majestic work of art exhibited from every room. The great room opened onto a large screened porch with steps leading down to a terrace, which housed a fireplace on one side and a fire pit on the other.

"These people like to build fires," Sam said.

He wrapped his arms around her from behind. "More fireplaces means better snuggling for us."

She leaned into him, comforted by the strength of his arms. "I think this place is perfect for us. Make your offer, but don't lowball so much you risk losing it. I can contribute the equity from my house once I sell it. And I have Mack's money if we need to use it for a down payment now."

A feeling of sadness swept through her as she thought of Captain Mack Bowman and how he had been like an uncle to the Sweeney sisters and their children. When he died unexpectedly last summer, he left his considerable wealth, which no one knew he had, to Sam, her sisters, and their mother.

Eli steered Sam up the brick steps. "Let's go talk to Sheila about our asking price."

While Eli consulted with the realtor in the kitchen, Sam stood by the wall of glass in the great room and watched a pelican dive for fish. She wrapped her arms around herself. *I could get used to this every morning.*

"Whoa!" Her older sister's high-pitched voice penetrated the silence. "Would you look at that view! Whose house is this?"

Sam spun around. "Maybe ours, if the owners accept our offer. What do you think?"

Jackie paraded around the room, sunglasses in hand, cashmere cape billowing out behind her. "I think it's amazing." She peeked in the kitchen, wiggling her fingers at Eli and the realtor, and then crossed the room to the master suite. "Appointed the right way, this house could be worthy of a magazine spread."

Sam laughed. "Giving credit to you as the designer?"

"Absolutely!" Jackie kissed the air beside Sam's ear. "I'll throw in my services for free, charging you only for any goods you purchase—furnishings and fabric and wall coverings.

Which, I'll warn you, could add up to a considerable amount. You realize your traditional furniture won't work in here, don't you? This room screams for elegant and sophisticated, fashioned in a comfortable style of course."

"Don't they call that shabby chic?"

"Uh . . . no. Shabby chic is so yesterday." Jackie flicked her wrist at Sam. "You might have to spend some of that money Mack left you. You can't buy a sports car like this and not put premium gas in it."

Sam held her palm out to silence her sister. "I get the picture already. What are you doing here anyway?"

"I have an early-afternoon appointment with a client in Charleston. I couldn't leave town until I congratulated you in person." Jackie moved to the window. "I hope you're prepared to have Faith as a neighbor. Her house is just three doors down that way." She pointed in the direction of the south. "I counted on my way in."

"I would love being neighbors with Faith, especially now that Annie is living with her."

Jackie grabbed Sam's hand and studied her engagement ring. "It's stunning, Sam. So old-fashioned."

"It belonged to Eli's grandmother."

"What a thoughtful gesture on his part. The ring suits you." Jackie lifted Sam's other hand and held them both wide. "The engagement suits you. Look at you. You're positively glowing."

Sam blushed. "Honestly, I didn't know it was possible to be this happy. And to think I almost threw it all away."

Jackie dropped Sam's hands. "But you didn't now, did you? Eli must be thrilled. Have you set a date yet?"

"We're thinking about Christmas Eve, a late-morning

service followed by a sit-down lunch for family and a few close friends."

"A Christmas wedding sounds charming. Would you like for me to call the club, to see if they have a private room available for the reception?"

Sam's eyes lit up. She'd been to the Prospect Country Club several times with Jackie. In addition to the eighteen-hole golf course, pool, and tennis courts, the property boasted a small clubhouse with expansive views of the inlet. "That would be perfect, if you don't mind."

"I'll call them first thing in the morning." Jackie circled Sam, eyeing her body from head to toe. "Christmas is four weeks away. You have a lot of decisions to make between now and then. Have you thought about what you're going to wear?"

Sam crossed her hands over her chest. "I haven't a clue, but I'll come up with something."

"Get real, Samantha. You're getting married. You can't just pull any old thing out of your closet for your wedding day. Long, white, and flowing is out of the question at your age, but you need something special. Can you come to Charleston this week? You can spend the night with me at the carriage house. We'll shop in the afternoon, and I'll take you to my new favorite restaurant for dinner."

"I wish I could, Jackie. But I can't afford your tastes. My credit cards have limits. I appreciate the offer though."

Jackie placed her hands on her hips. "I know you, little sister. You'll wait until the last minute, and then throw on some old rag you haven't worn in five years. We'll keep to your budget. I promise."

Sam inhaled a deep breath, and then let it out slowly. "I

guess you're right. If I want to look nice for Eli, I might as well take advantage of your impeccable style. We've been swamped at the market, but I can probably get away midweek."

Jackie removed her oversized iPhone from her hobo bag. "I have a lunch meeting on Tuesday, but if I juggle some appointments around, I can clear the rest of the afternoon and evening for you."

"Tuesday it is then." Sam took her sister by the elbow and walked her to the door.

"Good luck with your offer on the house. And give Eli a big hug for me. I'm so happy for you both." Jackie planted a kiss on Sam's cheek. "You deserve this, Samantha."

THREE

SAM AND ELI managed to finalize the terms, sign the offer to purchase the bungalow, and still make it to church on time. Jamie had walked the four blocks to church and was waiting for them in their usual pew. After the service, when they paused to speak to Reverend Webster on the front steps of the church, he'd already heard about their engagement.

"News sure travels fast around this town," Eli said, shaking the minister's hand.

Reverend Webster chuckled. "At the speed of the Internet."

"I'm surprised at you, Reverend," Eli said. "You don't seem the type to engage in social media."

"Not me." His turkey neck jiggled when he shook his head. "My wife is the junkie. She can't get enough. Facebook. Instagram. And that tweeter thingamajig." He turned to Sam. "Are you planning a fancy spring wedding like all the other newly engaged girls in town?"

"I'm hardly a girl, Reverend." She looped her arm

through her fiancé's. "Eli and I have waited long enough. We're contemplating a simple service and a small reception on Christmas Eve."

Frown lines creased the minister's forehead. "That might be somewhat of a challenge with the lineup of services we hold on Christmas Eve." He patted Sam's shoulder. "But don't you fret. Call the office in the morning, and we'll see what we can work out."

"That didn't sound very promising," Sam said on the way to the car.

"The First United Methodist Church of Prospect isn't the only place to get married," Eli said once they were all buckled in.

"Why not have the wedding out at Moss Creek Farm like Aunt Faith did?" Jamie said from the backseat.

The image of Jackie's spread of land, complete with waterfront acreage and an antebellum house, popped into Sam's head. She shifted in her seat to face her son. "That's a nice idea, Jamie. Jackie and Bill certainly have the space and have always been more than generous in opening their home to their family. But Faith's wedding was outside and the weather is too iffy to plan an outdoor wedding this time of year. I can't see us exchanging our vows in Jackie's living room."

"I agree with you there," Eli said as he started the car. "We'll figure something out. Right now, I'm starving. I need to get some food."

"Me too!" Jamie slapped the back of Eli's seat. "Let's go to brunch. Your engagement calls for a celebration."

Sam glanced at the clock on the dash. "I don't know if we have time for brunch, honey. I need you to help me put the lights up before you go back to school."

"No worries. I don't have to go back to school until late this afternoon."

"The Pelican's Roost it is then," Eli said, and put the car in gear.

❋

The Pelican's Roost was situated atop the Inlet View Marina. The red leather bench seats were cracked and worn, and the paneled walls housed a permanent odor of fried seafood; but the food was consistent and the view scenic with fishing boats coming and going from the docks below. Margie, the gray-haired waitress who'd worked at the Pelican's Roost for years, seated them at a table by the window and handed out menus.

"It's about time the two of you lovebirds decided to tie the knot," she said, chomping hard on the gum in her mouth. "I'm just so happy for y'all." She removed a pen from the brown bun on top of her head. "Today's special is mahi, cooked anyway you'd like it. We got all the breakfast fixings, plus a few lunch ones too, if you'd rather have the buffet. Can I start y'all off with something to drink? I recommend the mimosa since you're celebrating." She held her hand out to Jamie. "But I'll need to see your identification, young man."

Sam waved her off. "We're fine with just coffee."

Margie set cups and saucers in front of each of them and scurried off.

Leaning in, Jamie folded his arms on the table. "I'm proud of you, Mom, for not being tempted. How long have you been sober?"

She looked up from the menu. "A hundred and sixty-five days. And you better bet I'm tempted."

"You hide it well," Jamie said. "You seem like you're in a good place."

"I am in a good place, thanks to Eli." She ran her hand down Eli's thigh. "He makes me feel alive. I don't need chemical substances to dull my senses when I'm with him. I want to experience every moment and remember it in detail."

"What about you, Eli? How long has it been since you had a drink?" Eli stiffened and Jamie added, "I'm sorry. I didn't mean to get personal."

"I don't talk about my alcoholism to just anyone. But you're different, Jamie. You are going to be my stepson. If my past mistakes can help you avoid addiction problems in the future, I'm happy to share them with you. It's been five years and thirty-six days for me. And not a single one of them has been easy. But your mom is right. We find productive ways to spend our time. We take long walks. Go to the movies. Enjoy good food." He kissed Sam on the forehead. "And other things I'm not at liberty to discuss."

"Shh!" Sam held her finger to her lips. "Not in front of the child."

Jamie smiled. "Sitting around getting drunk every night is definitely a waste of time. But I have plenty of friends who do it. I don't drink that much. Mainly because I don't like being out of control. But I know a lot of people at school whose behavior borders on addictive. And I'm not just talking about drinking."

Sam squeezed her eyes shut, and then blinked them open again. "You mean drugs?" She contemplated the idea of her son living in a world where people used drugs. "I guess everyone smokes pot these days."

Jamie aimed his thumb at his chest. "Not me. I don't want to lose my baseball scholarship at USC," he said.

Eli stretched his arm out on the bench behind Sam. "You can come to either of us anytime, if you have a friend in crisis. We will always help, no questions asked."

Margie arrived with a carafe of coffee and filled their cups to the brim. She whipped out her notepad. "I'll start with the bride. What's it gonna be, honey?"

Sam closed her menu. "In the interest of time, I think we should have the buffet."

Jamie and Eli agreed, and they crossed the room to the buffet where they piled their plates high with scrambled eggs, sausage, grits, and biscuits from the covered casserole dishes on the buffet table. They returned to the table and dug in.

Sam spread her napkin on her lap. "What if we can't find a place to have the wedding?"

"Don't worry, sweetheart," Eli said, taking a bite of bacon. "We'll find a place. If you want to get married on Christmas Eve, we'll get married on Christmas Eve. Even if we have to get married here."

"Here? As in the Pelican's Roost?" She scrutinized the dingy dining room. "I don't think we're that desperate yet."

Eli shoveled up a forkful of eggs. "We live in the Lowcountry, one of the most romantic places in the United States. I'm sure we can find somewhere to have a wedding ceremony. What about one of the plantations? Surely they have a room they rent out for weddings."

Jamie slathered his biscuit with butter. "Or one of the old inns in Charleston?"

"Those are both great suggestions. But I was hoping to

find somewhere close to home. I'd hate to ask our family to travel on Christmas Eve."

"Why not?" Eli said. "Plenty of people travel over the holidays."

"Because . . ." Sam raked her fork around in her grits. "If market business is anything like it was at Thanksgiving, we will all be exhausted come December twenty-fourth. Maybe Christmas Eve is a bad idea. What about Valentine's Day?"

Jamie looked up from his plate. "Geez, Mom! That's downright corny."

"Have you considered your chapel?" Eli asked.

Sam dabbed at her mouth with her napkin. "Funny that you mention it. That's the first place I thought of. The simplicity of the sanctuary is what I admire most about the chapel, but I worry it might be too rustic for a wedding."

"Unpretentious sounds perfect to me," Eli said.

Sam dumped a packet of sweetener in her coffee. "I was christened and confirmed at First Methodist. I always thought I'd get married there."

Eli threw his hands up. "I'm just saying, if the Methodist church can't accommodate you, your Creekside Chapel might be a viable alternative."

Jamie took a bite of his biscuit. "Where is this chapel?"

"On the road to the beach, about five miles east of town," Sam said.

"How come you never took me there?"

"It's personal to me, one of those places that is hard to share." She sat back against the booth, sipping her coffee and thinking about the day she'd stumbled upon the quaint little chapel by the creek.

Two years ago, Jamie had suffered a severe spinal chord

injury in an ATV accident with his best friend on New Year's Day. Cory died on impact and Jamie was paralyzed from the waist down. In the agonizing months that followed, Sam watched her son mourn his best friend while he tried to cope with his physical challenges. Whenever she found a moment alone, she sought solace in her car, the only place she could hide her emotions from her family. One day in late February of that year, blinded by tears, Sam pulled off the highway into the nearest parking lot. Once she'd regained her composure, she realized she was parked in front of a white clapboard church she'd never known existed. Discovering the front door of the chapel unlocked, she slid into the second pew from the front and bowed her head in prayer. When she looked up sometime later, she was surprised to find an elderly gentleman sitting next to her. Sam returned many times to seek Pastor Paul's advice, even after Jamie regained the use of his legs. Paul's silvery voice set her at ease and his positive attitude toward life filled her with hope for the future.

❄

"Why don't we all fly down to Jamaica for Christmas?" Jamie suggested to Sam later that afternoon when they were putting lights up on the front of the house. "You and Eli could get married while the rest of us soak up the sun. Sophia wants to have a destination wedding. Tahiti or Maui, somewhere exotic."

Sam cleared her throat. "I'd like to meet this Sophia before you start planning the wedding."

She knew three things about Jamie's girlfriend. Sophia Rainey was a beautiful redhead from California who made her sorority her priority. Jamie had been seeing Sophia for eight months, but so far Sam had yet to meet her. As social chairman for her sorority, Sophia had been too busy organizing functions to join them for their tailgate parties at the Gamecock football games she and Eli had attended last fall.

"Get real, Mom! I don't mean *our* wedding. We've only been dating eight months. The subject of marriage has never come up. I'm just saying Sophia likes to travel. That's all."

Sam pulled another strand of lights from the plastic bin on the ground beside her. "Sad to think this might be the last year we put lights up on our little yellow house. We've been doing this since you were in kindergarten."

"Just think, though. Next Christmas, if we buy the bungalow, we can enter the dock parade just like all the other houses on the creek. We'll have to decide whether to go with elegant or tacky decorations for our dock. Maybe tacky, since Aunt Jackie usually wins Best Tree with her twelve-foot artificial fir and all its thousands of little white blinking lights."

"That could be fun. We could collaborate our efforts with Faith and Mike." Sam paused as she finished draping her light over the porch railing. "Sounds like you're as excited as Eli and I are about the idea of buying this house."

"Are you kidding me? The place rocks. You know I've always wanted to live on the inlet."

Sam straightened. "So you're okay with all this. I mean the wedding and everything happening so fast?"

"If I had my way, you'd already be married." Jamie plugged the extension cord into the outlet on the porch and stood back to admire their handiwork. Icicle lights hung from the eaves of the house, strands of blinking lights outlined the porch, and nets of lights covered the foundation shrubs.

They stacked the plastic bins and carried them inside. "I

wish you didn't have to leave," Sam said. "I've enjoyed having you home, and I appreciate you helping out at the market. We wouldn't have made it on Wednesday without you."

"I'll be back in three weeks. You can count on me to work overtime during my break. I need to earn some money." He dropped the plastic bins in the corner of the sitting room with the rest of the decorations. "You'll wait for me to do the tree, won't you?"

She mussed his hair. "Of course. It'll be our last tree together, just you and me."

He plopped down on the sofa and stared up at the ceiling. "Where would we put the Christmas tree in our new house?"

"Stop talking about it," she said, hands on hips. "You'll jinx our offer."

"Don't be so superstitious, and have a little faith. The way I see it, we have lots of options of where to put the tree. It might be cool to put it in the center of the room." He hopped up off the sofa. "Imagine this." He spread his hands in the air in front of them. "Us, drinking hot chocolate and opening gifts in leather chairs arranged around a ten-foot tree with tons of ornaments and twinkling lights."

Sam closed her eyes as she imagined the scene. "Strangely enough, I can see the tree in the center of the great room. The bungalow definitely defies tradition."

"Which is exactly why it's so perfect for our family."

FOUR

WHEN THE OWNERS of the bungalow made a counteroffer on Sunday evening, Sam and Eli stayed up well past midnight juggling their finances and pooling their resources in order to counter the counter, a proposal that split the difference with the owners. Sam dragged herself into work on Monday in anticipation of the busy weeks ahead.

In the back office late morning, Sam and Faith were reworking their catering menu to include items their customers requested the most at Christmas—beef tenderloin, eggnog cheesecake, and oyster stew. Sam dropped her pen on the desk and buried her face in her hands. "Maybe it's too much to have this wedding on Christmas Eve. It seemed like a good idea at the time, and I don't like the idea of having to wait until spring. All I really want is to be married to Eli. But with business the way it's been . . ."

Faith looked up from the menu. "It's not like you to give up so easily. Where's the Sammie spunk we all admire?

Christmas Eve is family time, the perfect time to get married in my opinion. If we all pitch in, we can make it happen."

"I don't know how, unless you can come up with a church and a place for the reception. The secretary at First Methodist says they have no room in their schedule for a wedding on Christmas Eve. And Jackie just texted me that all the private banquet rooms at the club are booked on December twenty-fourth."

"So find another venue." Faith leaned back in her chair and sipped her coffee. "What about getting married at the farm like I did?"

"I can't ask Jackie to do that on Christmas Eve."

"Why not? She's already having our family dinner that night. Start the party a little earlier, throw in a minister, and we've got ourselves a wedding."

"And just where do you suggest I find a minister who won't be holding Christmas Eve services for his parishioners?"

"Oh. I hadn't thought of that." Faith crossed her arms and stared up at the ceiling. "What about your little chapel?"

Sam's mouth fell open. "How'd you know about the chapel?"

Faith grinned. "I've seen your Jeep there a time or two. I figured you would have told me about it if you'd wanted me to know."

Sam picked up her pen. "The chapel might work. I'll drive out there this afternoon and talk to Pastor Paul."

Annie arrived around three thirty for her after-school shift. "I really want to help you with the wedding," she said, tying a green apron around her waist. "Whatever you need. Food. Flowers. Name it."

"I accept your offer. The way the phone's been ringing off

the hook here today, we're in for a busy few weeks. I'm going to need all the help I can get to pull this wedding together."

Sam studied the sixteen-year-old girl opposite the fish counter from her. She'd changed a lot from the waif who'd arrived on their doorstep six months ago posing as a teenager down on her luck. Annie had come to Prospect with an agenda. She needed a slice of Jamie's liver in order to save her father's life. Their father's life. Allen Bethune. The man who had abandoned Sam when she found out she was pregnant with Jamie. He died before the doctors could make a decision about the transplant. With her biological mother out of the picture, the young girl was suddenly all alone in the world. Even though Annie lived with Faith, all three Sweeney sisters as well as their mother felt responsible for helping raise her.

Sam eyed the girl suspiciously. "What's different about you?" Annie no longer resembled a scrawny baby bird with matted feathers but an exotic mermaid with shiny golden hair and curves in all the right places.

"I'm getting fat, that's what. I've gained ten pounds and it's all right here." She smacked her butt.

"You look great. You needed to gain some weight. But that's not it. There's something else, something that's not physical." Sam's mouth fell open and her eyes grew wide. "Do you have a boyfriend?"

Annie's cheeks turned a vibrant shade of pink.

"You do!" Sam clasped her hands together. "You have a boyfriend."

"Shh!" Annie cast a quick glance around the room, to make certain they were alone. "Promise me you won't tell anyone. We're still in the early stages."

"I won't say anything." Sam leaned across the fish counter. "As long as you tell me who the lucky guy is."

Annie shook her head. "I can't do that. Not yet. But you'll be the first to know if and when we officially become a couple."

"Okay, fine. But you make sure he's good to you." She wagged her finger at Annie. "You're a nice girl. You deserve to be treated with kindness and respect."

"Don't worry, Sam. I grew up with my father's deadbeat friends. I know a good guy when I see one."

"I'm sure you do." Sam dared to imagine what Annie's life had been like as the daughter of a fisherman, moving from one marina to the next in Florida and the Keys. Not an easy life for a little girl and her single-parent father. The life Sam and Jamie would have had if she'd married Allen all those years ago.

"Okay then." Sam straightened, holding her shoulders back and her head high. "Wish me luck. I'm going to see a pastor about a chapel."

※

The sun had already begun its descent over the inlet in the bleak winter sky when Sam pulled into the gravel lot at the Creekside Chapel. She wrapped her Barbour tight around her as she dashed from the car to the chapel. She took her usual seat in the second pew and bowed her head, offering thanks to God for the blessings in her life and asking him for patience in dealing with her shortcomings. The scent of mothballs alerted her to Pastor Paul's presence. She opened her eyes to find him sitting next to her, wearing his clerical collar and shirt beneath an old gray cardigan.

"How are you, my dear?" he said in his melodic voice. "It's been awhile."

"I know, Pastor, and I'm sorry. I'm not going to make excuses for myself, except to say that, while I haven't been to see you, I've attended services nearly every Sunday at First Methodist."

He nodded his approval. "As long as you're getting your fix somewhere." He smiled at his own joke.

"I've never thought to ask. Do you have services here?"

"As a matter of fact, we do." Placing his arm on the back of the pew, Pastor Paul turned in his seat to face Sam. "Nine o'clock service every Sunday morning in the summer and five o'clock on Sunday evenings during the rest of the year. All our services are casual, come-as-you-are affairs."

"Does anyone ever get married here?"

"All the time. Young folks like our laid-back atmosphere. Sometimes I conduct the ceremony; other times they bring in their own minister. The chapel belongs to the people of the inlet. Whatever works for them is fine with us." He chuckled. "Of course, the only *us* here is me. There is no other staff."

Out of obligation to her mother, and because that's all she'd known growing up, Sam attended services two weeks a month at First Methodist. But she felt her real connection to God here, in this simple clapboard chapel with its windows that looked out over the inlet. Who needed stained glass with God's handiwork in plain sight? It felt right for her to pledge her love to Eli here.

"Would you consider marrying me, Pastor Paul?" She held out her left hand. "I got engaged over the weekend. I'm crazy about him."

A soft smile parted the old man's lips. "Eli, I presume."

She'd only visited the chapel a handful of times, yet Pastor Paul knew her better than Reverend Webster ever would. "Eli is a police officer. I can't wait for you to meet him. I think the two of you will hit it off." She drew in a deep breath. "The thing is, we really have our hearts set on getting married Christmas Eve. Just a simple service, family only, late morning, followed by a sit-down lunch. That is, if I can find a place to have the reception. I hope you'll join us. For the luncheon, I mean. If you're free of course. And if the chapel isn't being used for services." She paused to breathe. "I should probably shut up now."

He patted her hand. "I would be delighted to marry you, Samantha, on Christmas Eve or any other day you choose."

"Really?" she asked, and he nodded. "Really."

She slumped back against the pew. "That's wonderful, Pastor. This place is very special to me. I think I was meant to get married here."

Sam tried to imagine the scene. She, wearing a dress of some sort–that part was blurry—standing at the altar with Eli, surrounded by dozens of white poinsettias, her family in attendance in the congregation. "Would it be okay if we brought in flowers?"

"Of course. Flowers are one of the Lord's many gifts to us." He placed his hands, fingers splayed, on his thighs. "So when do I get to meet Eli?"

"Whenever it's convenient for you. Should I schedule an appointment with your secretary?" Sam asked, her periwinkle eyes full of mischief.

His laughter echoed throughout the sanctuary. "You'd be hard pressed to get in touch with her. Stop by anytime. I'm always here."

✷

Eli called Sam on her way home with the news that the sellers had agreed to their counteroffer and the contract had been signed.

Sam punched the air. "Woo-hoo! Our luck is turning. We have a chapel and a house. Now all we have left to do is find a place for a reception."

"According to Sheila, the owners are having some sort of crisis. Personal or financial, she didn't say. But they are pushing us to close the house by the end of the year."

"Can we make it happen that fast?" Sam asked.

"Our loan officer at the bank has assured me that it's not a problem, but I have to admit, it makes me kind of nervous."

Sam drummed her fingers on the steering wheel. "Nervous? It scares the hell out of me. Especially with everything else we have going on. But don't listen to me. We all know how much I dislike change."

FIVE

SAM ARRIVED IN Charleston at Jackie's carriage house, the temporary offices of JSH Designs, as she was finishing up with her noon appointment. "Why don't you wait for me inside where it's cool?" Jackie held the front door open for Sam. "I'm going to walk Marcie to her car, and I'll be back in a minute." The two women tromped off down the garden path, their arms loaded with sample books of fabric and wallpaper.

Sam crossed the threshold and stepped back into the nineteenth century to the pre-Civil War days when the carriage house was used to store horse-drawn carriages. Exposed beams ran the length of the ceiling, while oak planks in random widths, worn from age, covered the floors. Dappled sunlight beamed in through the arched windows on either side of the main room, both sides having formerly been open to allow entry for the carriages. More sample books and carpet swatches covered every available surface of the room. The floor, the tables, and even the mantel above the small stone fireplace—all piled high with books. Two young women, not long out of college, sat on either side of a conference table, each with a phone pressed to her ear, sample books and notepads scattered on the table in front of them.

The woman with long, silky black hair held the phone to her chest. "Make yourself at home." She eyed the overnight bag in Sam's hand. "You can put that upstairs if you'd like."

Sam mouthed her thanks and climbed the stairs to the second floor. A double bed dominated the majority of the space in the lone bedroom. Sam had not slept in the same bed with her sister since they were girls.

This should be interesting. I wonder if she snores.

She pulled off her Sweeney's Market polo and slipped on a long-sleeve gray blouse. Taking her toiletries bag to the tiny bathroom next door, she quickly brushed through her cropped hair and smeared on a thin coat of pale pink lipstick. She then slipped her coat on and returned to the office downstairs.

Jackie was waiting for her. Sam gave her sister a half-hug. "I hope you're making headway in your search for office space, because it looks to me like you're busting at the seams here."

Jackie cocked back her meticulously coiffed dark head and laughed. "The quarters are so cramped it's a wonder the three of us don't kill each other." She motioned to her staff. "Liza, Cecilia, this is my sister Sam." Still clutching their phones, the girls poked their heads up from their work and waved.

Jackie placed a hand on a stack of neatly folded fabric samples on the conference table. "These are for you, for the bungalow. I had the girls pull them this morning. We'll look at them after dinner if you'd like."

"So you're forcing me into putting premium gas in the Cadillac I just bought?"

"Damn straight. Just like I'm forcing you into buying a wedding dress. As your older sister, it's my job to set you straight."

"Huh! As your younger sister, it's my job not to listen to you."

"Are you hungry? I have some oriental chicken salad left over from my lunch with Marcie."

"Thanks, but I stopped in at Chick-fil-A on the way here."

"Then what're we waiting for?" Jackie retrieved her hobo bag from her desk and led Sam out the front door. "Before we hit the shops, I want to show you my new project." She marched Sam across the garden path to the side porch of a two-story Federal-style house, the main residence on the property. Jackie unlocked the back door and they entered a galley kitchen. "I have an architect working on designs to expand this room into the backyard. Other than gutting the bathrooms upstairs and reconfiguring a few of the closets, the rest of the work needed is cosmetic."

Sam followed her sister throughout the downstairs, from the generous-size dining and living rooms at the front of the house down the wide center hallway to the library and sunroom at the back. She ran her hand along the mahogany banister on the handsome curving staircase. "What're you planning to do with it when you're finished, sell it?"

"Eventually. But not for a while. For now I'm going to use the house to showcase my work." Jackie held her arms wide as she glided down the center hall. "Don't you think it'll be a wonderful place to entertain potential clients?"

"Every woman in Charleston will be beating down your door to get a glimpse inside this house. I've got to hand it to you, Jack. Your hard work is paying off." Sam regarded her sister's attire—black leggings, tall boots, and a thigh-length camel-colored sweater. "You certainly look the part of the New York professional. Are you going to be embarrassed to be seen with me?"

Jackie gave Sam the quick once-over. "Not at all. But you don't need this." She helped Sam out of her coat. "It's warm outside. And your hair is too flat." She mussed Sam's hair, tucking a stray strand behind her left ear. "There now. Let's go hit the shops."

❋

Sam and Jackie moseyed in and out of the boutiques on and around King Street. She tried on dresses, suits, skirts, and blouses. The clothes were either too dressy, too casual, or cut in a style unflattering to her slight figure. Jackie insisted she find something in winter white, but Sam wasn't sold on one particular color, although she didn't think a bride should wear black regardless of her age. It was nearing five o'clock and Sam's stomach was beginning to rumble when Jackie grabbed her by the arm and dragged her down a narrow side street. She stopped in front of a building that looked more like a house than a storefront. Jackie pressed the buzzer beside the red front door.

"Who lives here?" Sam asked.

"Nobody. It's a boutique."

"Why do they keep their doors locked? Doesn't that defeat the purpose of welcoming customers?" Sam glanced up and down the street. "Or are they worried they might get robbed?"

"There's always that chance in downtown Charleston.

But that's not the reason. Marguerite only sees clients by appointment."

Sam jabbed an elbow in her sister's side. "You shanghaied me. I won't be able to afford a pair of panties in a place like this."

Jackie grinned. "So spend some of Mack's money."

Marguerite spoke with a French accent, although Sam was fairly certain she was Spanish. Sam guessed her to be in her midforties. With dark features, she posed a striking figure in a red knit suit that complimented her slim build. She spun Sam around, studying her from every angle. "Very nice. I have several things in mind that might work." She showed them to a sitting area outside of the dressing room. "Please, have a seat. Can I offer you a glass of wine while you wait?" Jackie and Sam declined. "Then I'll gather some selections and be back in a flash." She clicked off across the marble floor in her stiletto boots.

Sam tried on ten different ensembles, all impeccably tailored in an assortment of fabrics in various shades of winter white. She quickly narrowed her choice to three. A two-piece suit with a lace jacket and A-line skirt. A pair of wide-legged wool slacks, sheer silk blouse, and long cashmere cardigan. And a long-sleeved simple-cut dress with a double row of silver grommets along the bottom.

When Sam emerged from the dressing room in the dress, Jackie said, "That's the one."

"I agree," Marguerite said, and rushed to Sam's side. "This is exquisite on you. Perfect for a mature bride. We'll take in a little along the sides, here and here." She pinched the fabric at Sam's breasts and hips. "You can wear high-heeled tall black boots or a sexy sandal, silver perhaps, with bare legs."

"Whatever you do, don't wear those," Jackie said, her eyes on Sam's cowboy boots.

"Duh," Sam said, laughing. "The floor is cold. I didn't want to come out here barefoot."

"Do you really think this is it?" Sam asked her sister. "It's more than I planned to spend."

"Absolutely. You only get married once. I hope that's the case, anyway, at your age." Jackie winked at her in the mirror. "Nothing would make Mack happier than to know he'd paid for your wedding dress. He so wanted you to marry Eli."

"In that case, I'll buy the slacks ensemble as well, to wear for my going-away outfit."

"Even if the only place you're going is my Christmas Eve party at the farm."

❄

It was approaching six thirty, and Sam and Jackie were both starving by the time Marguerite finished pinning for the alterations. "I made a seven o'clock reservation at Slightly North of Broad," Jackie said on the way back to the car. "Have you ever eaten there? The food is over the top."

"No, but I've heard plenty about it."

The hostess seated them in a quiet corner of the restaurant. Jackie ordered a glass of Malbec and Sam a nonalcoholic beer. Over heirloom tomato salads followed by shrimp and grits, the sisters discussed Sam's options of places to hold her wedding reception.

"The Pelican's Roost will have to do," Sam said, draining the last of her O'Doul's. "There's no place else to have it."

"Hold on a minute. Let's not give up so easily." Jackie sat

back in her chair, wine glass in hand. "When are you closing on your house?"

"We don't have an exact date yet. But it will be before the end of the year. Why?"

"Is there any chance you can take possession of the house before the twenty-fourth?"

"Maybe," Sam said. "What are you thinking?"

Jackie tipped her wine glass at Sam. "I'm thinking you should have the reception at the bungalow. Hire a caterer, rent a couple of tables, and voila, instant party. You certainly can't beat the view."

Sam gnawed on her lip as she tried to imagine the scene. Fires crackling in both fireplaces. A Christmas tree in the corner by the windows. A long table decked out in linen and china in the center of the great room. Soft Christmas music playing over the music system. Snow falling outside. Except that it hardly ever snowed in the Lowcountry. "It could work."

"It could work, hell. It's a brilliant idea and you know it."

"How will I find a caterer willing to work on Christmas Eve?"

"You really are so naive sometimes, Samantha. People in the catering business do their celebrating after Christmas. Servers, cooks, and bartenders all work on holidays. Finding a caterer willing to plan your reception on Christmas Eve is not a problem. But finding a decent caterer who lives in Prospect is. Trust me, I know. I've tried them all. Let me make a few calls. I should have someone for you by the end of the week."

SIX

TRUE TO HER word, Jackie came up with a caterer for Sam. Heidi Butler called Sam around lunchtime on Thursday to schedule a meeting.

In one long breath, Heidi said, "Your sister suggested I give you a call, that you are looking for someone to cater your wedding luncheon on Christmas Eve. I would love to meet with you and give you a proposal if you're interested. I have a long list of referrals. Unfortunately, they all live in Beverly Hills. I am working on establishing my reputation locally. I'm willing to cater your party at cost in exchange for you allowing me to photograph the job. Jackie says your bungalow is charming."

Beverly Hills? At cost? Who is this woman?

"That's a very generous offer, Heidi, but let's back up for a minute. How do you know my sister?"

"As a newcomer to the area, I've been introducing myself to the top interior designers. Decorators know all the right people in town, the ones that have the money to spend on making their homes beautiful and elaborate parties to entertain their friends."

Sam laughed out loud. "That's a wise strategy if ever I heard one." She gave Heidi the address to the market and agreed to meet with her the following afternoon.

Sam took an instant liking to the caterer when she arrived a few minutes after three, early for their three thirty appointment. She had white-blonde hair piled atop her head and a heart-shaped face with thin rosy lips, heavy eyelashes, and emerald eyes that sparkled with life. Dressed in slim-fitting black pants and a tailored white cotton blouse, Heidi teetered about the showroom on three-inch black pumps.

"I brought you samples of my cuisine." She set a large picnic basket on the counter and lifted the lid. She removed foil-wrapped packages and plastic containers of sweet potato ham biscuits, lamb chops, spring rolls, deviled eggs, and an assortment of bite-size tarts.

"Goodness, Heidi, there's enough food here for ten wedding receptions." Sam's stomach growled. "But don't mind if I do. I haven't eaten anything since a bowl of Special K at breakfast." She reached for a lamb chop. The tender meat, flavored with rosemary and thyme, was delicious, and she gnawed it to the bone. "That was really good." She tossed the bone into the trash can and picked up another lamb chop.

Lovie came out from the kitchen with a tray of stone crab claws. She slid the tray into the cooler. "What's all this?" she asked when she saw the spread of food on the counter.

"Mom, this is Heidi Butler, the caterer I was telling you about from Charleston. Heidi, this is my mother, Lovie."

Heidi extended her hand toward Lovie. "I've heard a lot

about you from Jackie. I understand you're the connoisseur of seafood. I have some big shoes to fill."

"Connoisseur of seafood? That's a new one on me, a distinction I'm not sure I deserve. But thank you just the same." Lovie selected a deviled egg from the tray and nibbled at the white part.

Sam sampled the spring rolls. "Your food is delicious. No doubt about it. But I noticed you didn't bring any seafood with you. I have to warn you, Heidi, the Sweeneys never order from the landlubber's menu. Everything at the reception will come from the sea. I hope that's not a problem for you."

"No problem at all." Heidi excused Sam's concerns with a flick of her wrist. "In fact, seafood is one of my specialties. I can cook it any way you like it. But I thought it best for us to get to know one another before I showed you up."

Lovie burst out laughing, nearly choking on her deviled egg.

Sam pointed her spring roll at Heidi. "I like this girl. We're gonna get along just fine." She glanced at the ship's clock above the door. "The realtor is supposed to meet us in ten minutes to let us in the house, but I don't want to leave until my afternoon shift arrives. I don't want Mom to be alone, not with the crazy business we've had all week."

"That sounds like a good problem to have. Are you offering your customers anything special for the holidays?"

Sam set one of the flyers she'd printed with their holiday menu on the counter. "In addition to the casseroles and desserts we've offered in the past, this year we've added a variety of meats." She pointed at the flyer. "Beef tenderloin. Roasts. Organic, free-range turkeys. And country hams from Virginia."

Heidi removed a pair of cat eye reading glasses from her bag and scanned the menu. "You've created a comprehensive list. By including items other than seafood, you've made Sweeney's a one-stop shop for your customers. Lucky for you and me, more and more people seem to be ordering out instead of cooking themselves. The holidays—"

Heidi fell silent when Annie came flying through the door.

Out of breath, with hair stuck to her face, Annie dropped her backpack at her feet. "I'm so sorry I'm late. My English teacher kept us after the bell. We spent the last part of class going over the essay questions for our exam. I couldn't just leave."

"Of course not. Your school work comes first." Sam introduced Annie to the caterer.

"Your stepdaughter?" Heidi asked. "Jackie told me you'd never been married?"

Her skin prickled. *What else had Jackie told this stranger about her?* Sam waved her off. "It's a long story. Suffice it to say, we don't get hung up on technicalities around here."

Lovie winked at Annie. "Family is family, regardless of whether a marriage license exists or the DNA matches."

Sam moved to Annie's side. "You're looking at a future winner of *Top Chef*," she said, draping her arm around the girl's shoulders. "Annie would like to be a part of the wedding preparations, and I have given her the authority to make decisions regarding food and decorations on my behalf."

Annie beamed.

"In that case, why don't you email me and we can start bouncing some ideas around." Heidi fished a business card out of her bag and handed it to Annie.

"Let's not get ahead of ourselves," Sam said. "We need to agree on the price first."

Annie took the card and shoved it into her pocket. "I'll let the two of you work that out. I'm starving. I hope you don't mind." She popped a pecan tart in her mouth and closed her eyes as she savored it. "This is really good." She licked her lips. "But next time, you should consider adding a hint of chocolate."

※

Heidi followed Sam the short distance to the bungalow in her classic antique Mustang convertible. The car was a sleek-looking machine, a turquoise jewel, but Sam thought it could use a tune-up based on the spitting and sputtering it made on the way through town.

The realtor was waiting for them in the driveway in front of the bungalow. "I'm sorry we're late," Sam said. "I got held up at the market."

"No worries. I used the extra time to work on a contract for a client." She unlocked the front door for them. "Have a look around. I'll be in my car if you need me."

Heidi waltzed in and began taking pictures of the great room with her iPhone. "This space is incredible, Sam. The natural light is ethereal." She moved to the window. "With this view, who needs decorations? You can do as much or as little as you'd like for the luncheon."

Sam suddenly found it difficult to breathe. "What I'd like is for you and Annie to surprise me." She joined Heidi at the window. "I'm feeling overwhelmed with the increase in business at the market, not to mention getting married and moving and the normal stresses of the holidays. I'm probably the only bride in the world who willingly relinquishes control of the single most important event in her life. But right now, all I want is to be married to the man I love and settled in the house of my dreams."

Heidi turned to face her. "Then you've found the right girl. My clients in Beverly Hills never had time for planning parties. Even when they had the time, they wanted someone else to do everything for them." She removed her iPad from her bag. "Do you mind looking through a few photographs so I can get an idea of your tastes?"

"Not at all." Sam took the iPad from her and for the next few minutes, they scrolled through images of the elaborate affairs Heidi had conceived and executed at her previous job in Beverly Hills.

Sam handed back the iPad. "You do lovely work, Heidi. Problem is, I'm not sure I can afford Beverly Hills prices, even with the discount you mentioned."

"I'm not offering you a discount, Sam. I'm offering to do this party for you at cost in exchange for you letting me photograph the reception for my website. This is a business arrangement where we both get something we want."

Sam looked away. "I don't know how I feel about having my face plastered all over your website."

"No offense. Your face is stunning." Heidi smiled. "But I'm more interested in photographs of the food and venue. I promise not to post any pictures of the attendees or the guests of honor."

Sam felt the tension leave her body. "Then how can I say no? I'd be a fool to turn down a deal like that." She held out her hand and they shook to seal the deal.

They spoke briefly about the details as Sam walked Heidi

to her car. She watched the antique Mustang hiccup down the driveway before tapping on Sheila's window.

Sheila opened her car door. "All finished."

"Inside, yes. But I was wondering if you have a minute. I could use some real estate advice."

Sheila placed her files in the passenger seat and got out of the car to face her. "How can I help?"

"The news about us buying the bungalow has spread around town, and several people have expressed an interest in my house on Dogwood Lane. I was thinking of holding a soft"—she used air quotes—"open house on Sunday. Problem is, I have no idea how to go about showing a house."

"In order for me to get involved, you would need to sign a listing agreement. Is that something you would consider?"

"Of course. I have no problem with that at all," Sam said.

"In that case, we can try the open house. But I warn you that December is a difficult time of year to sell a house, even in this seller's market. If you don't get any offers, we can put it in the MLS listing after the first of the year and start an aggressive advertising campaign. I'll draw up the paperwork and bring it with me on Sunday." Sheila started toward her car, and then turned back around. "I trust your house is in good shape. No peeling paint, leaking faucets, or messy closets."

Sam gulped. "No worries. What's broken now will be fixed by Sunday."

SEVEN

SAM STOPPED FAITH as she was leaving the market at noon on Friday. "I hate to ask you this, but is there any way you can cover my shift tomorrow? I have a million things I need to do at home before the open house on Sunday."

Sam cringed with guilt, knowing that Faith managed the accounting for the market and seldom worked the showroom. But even more important, Faith's duties freed up her afternoons and weekends to spend with her young daughter and new husband.

Faith closed the back door against the cold. "I'd be happy to help you out."

"Are you sure? I know how sacred your weekends are."

"I'm sure. Mike has the weekend off from the hospital. But he and Bitsy are so wrapped up in their decorations for the dock parade they hardly know I'm around."

Sam gave her sister's arm a quick rub. "Thank you. Normally I wouldn't worry about Annie and Mom being here alone, but this week has been crazy. I think everyone in town is having a party this year."

"That's a good problem for us to have."

"Do you have any idea what Bitsy and Mike are planning for the parade?"

"None. They're keeping it top secret." Faith fumbled in her purse for her keys. "Did Jackie mention Friday night to you? Bill has offered to take all of us in his boat for the parade. And Mike and I are having everyone over for chili afterward. I hope you and Eli will join us."

Sam smiled. "I wouldn't miss it. Thanks for including us. It'll give me something to look forward to."

Sam spent the day on Saturday, cleaning out closets and cabinets and under beds. She vacuumed, dusted, and polished until every surface shined. She scrubbed the tile in the bathroom and cleaned the bugs and cobwebs from the light fixtures on the front porch and back deck. When Eli got off work at three, they oiled door hinges, replaced burned-out spotlights outside, and fixed the toilet in Jamie's bath that continued to run even after the bowl had filled.

Five of the six people Sam invited to the open house on Sunday agreed to come. Sam left Sheila in charge of showing the house while she spent that afternoon at the market, organizing their special orders for Christmas and adjusting her inventory for the increase in business during the weeks ahead. By the time she-returned home at six o'clock, three of the five potential buyers had made offers. One of them, a young police officer who worked with Eli at the station, made a considerably higher offer than the other two.

"His wife is expecting a baby in late January," Shiela explained. "They've been looking for a house for almost a year. For financial reasons, they can't close until mid-January, but they'd like to move in right after Christmas and pay you rent for the following month. The lease on their apartment is up on December 31. Obviously, they don't want to renew. And they'd like to get settled before the baby comes."

"I don't know," Sam said, her lips pressed into a fine line. "I was hoping we could take our time in moving into the bungalow."

"Why don't you give us a chance to discuss the offer?" Eli said as he escorted Sheila to the door. "We'll call you in a little while."

He closed the door behind the realtor, and crossed the sitting room to Sam. "I realize this is a lot on you at once," he said, taking her in his arms. "But I don't see how we can leave that much money on the table. The other two offers are ten thousand dollars less. Do you know what we can do with ten thousand dollars? We'll make it work somehow. I promise."

Sam rested her head on his shoulder. "I'll remind you of that on December twenty-fourth when we are getting married, moving into a new house, and celebrating Christmas all in one weekend."

"I'm not saying it'll be perfect. But I can promise we'll get it all done." He kissed her hair. "This is a happy time for us. Why don't we go to dinner to celebrate?"

"I don't feel much like celebrating. I know I should be ecstatic, selling my house without officially putting it on the market, but I can't shake this nagging feeling that something is wrong."

He held her at arm's length. "You're not getting cold feet, are you?"

"About marrying you? Never." She cupped his cheek.

"Just a lot of changes at once for a girl like me who has worn the same pair of cowboy boots for the past fifteen years."

While Eli called the realtor to accept the pregnant couple's offer, Sam wandered from room to room, remembering the events that had taken place in her yellow Cape Cod during the past eighteen years. Her tour down Memory Lane ended in the kitchen where she removed a pint of barbecue from the freezer, brewed a cup of peppermint tea, and called Jamie with the news.

"That's awesome! Does this mean we can move into the house sooner?"

"Aren't you the least bit sad? I just sold our home."

"Stop being so sentimental, Mom. The bungalow rocks."

Get a grip, Sam. Everyone is excited about this move except you.

"I've been meaning to call you," Jamie said, his tone more serious. "I hope you don't mind, but I invited Sophia to come home with me for Christmas."

"You did what?!" Sam said, slumping back against the counter.

A stranger in the house for Christmas? As if we don't already have enough going on.

"Her parents accepted a last-minute invitation to go to Russia for the holidays. I didn't want Sophia to be alone, especially not at Christmas."

Right. The fourth thing Sam knew about Sophia—she was an only child like Jamie.

Sam sighed. "Of course not. Do you know how long she's planning to stay? I'm going to need your help with the move. We have to be out of this house by the twenty-eighth."

"I'm sure she'll be gone by then," Jamie said, but Sam didn't think her son sounded so sure at all.

Over dinner, Sam broke the news to Eli about Sophia. "I've been dying to meet her, just not in the middle of our chaos."

"We're getting married, honey. In my book, the more family and friends who attend the wedding the merrier. Besides, throwing Sophia into our *chaos* will show us what she's made of. If she's anything like Annie, she'll jump right in and make herself useful."

Sam felt a glimmer of hope. Eli was right. When Annie first came to town, she dove headfirst into their lives and landed on both feet. She was an asset to all of them at every turn—in the kitchen, at the market, with Bitsy. Maybe they'd get lucky. Maybe Sophia would turn out to be as equally helpful and pleasant as Annie to be around.

EIGHT

SAM HAD LITTLE free time outside of work that week, aside from the few minutes of online Christmas shopping she managed before falling exhausted into bed at night. The phone at Sweeney's rang all day long with special orders for Christmas and the weekends in between. Business was booming. And she needed to stay focused.

Not so long ago, eighteen months if anyone was counting, Captain Sweeney's Seafood had almost gone bankrupt. Renovations to modernize the market had been an unpopular move with the local crowd, and the Sweeney family was forced to prove themselves all over again. Sam's wasn't the only livelihood that relied upon the market's success. Both Lovie and Faith depended on their steady incomes. And although Jamie hadn't made up his mind for certain yet, she sensed he was interested in running the business after he graduated from college.

On Friday night, Mike and Bitsy won first prize in the boat parade for their dock decorations. Which included, but was not limited to, Santa in his sleigh guided by a team of reindeer prancing down the dock railing preparing for takeoff. With Bitsy's help, Mike had spent months constructing and painting the plywood props and outlining them with strands of lights. Sam had never witnessed a happier seven-year-old than Bitsy when she accepted her trophy from the mayor.

Annie and Cooper, one of Jackie's seventeen-year-old twins, could not take their eyes off of one another during the celebration at Faith's house afterward.

Is he the mystery boy responsible for Annie's glow?

Sam's suspicions were confirmed the following day when she happened upon the two of them huddled together, whispering and giggling, in the corner of the kitchen at Sweeney's.

"Cooper, honey, you're just the guy I'm looking for." Sam made herself busy at the sink, cleaning out a shrimp steamer. "Oysters are in hot demand these days. We've already gone through the bushels you brought in on Wednesday. Is there any chance I can persuade you and Sean to go for more?"

"We're already on it, Aunt Sam. I'm waiting for Sean to pick me up. He went out to the farm to get some buckets."

"You're a godsend. I don't know what I'll do when the two of you leave for college in the fall."

Based on the crestfallen look on her face, Annie was dreading his departure as well.

Sam waited for Cooper to leave before confronting Annie. "Cooper's the one, isn't he?"

"The one who what?" Annie said, narrowing her eyes.

Sam wagged her finger at the girl. "Don't play dumb with me, missy. I know he's the one responsible for that extra kick in your step."

Annie's cheeks grew pink. "Please don't say anything to

anybody. Neither of us has ever been in a relationship before. It's all so new. We agreed to take things slow."

Sam set the steamer pot in the rack to drain. "Don't worry. Your secret is safe with me." Moving down the counter, she gathered a cutting board and utility knife, and began dicing potatoes. "How does Sean feel about your relationship?"

Cooper and Sean had quite literally fought for Annie's attention last summer when she first came to town. Jackie had come home from Charleston to find them duking it out in the backyard. At the time, Annie had been more interested in saving her father's life than in a relationship with either of the twins.

Annie grabbed a knife and an onion and joined Sam at the counter. "Sean doesn't know about Cooper and me yet. At least I don't think so. I'm never really sure what goes on between those two. You know, that eerie twin thing?"

Sam smiled. "I know it well."

Annie brushed an onion tear off her cheek with the back of her hand. "Anyway, Sean has a girlfriend. I like her a lot. Her name is Mindy, and she's really pretty with an awesome haircut, short and blonde, like yours."

Sam nudged Annie with her elbow. "Make Cooper be good to you. And don't let him talk you into doing anything you're not ready to do."

Annie blushed again. "Don't worry, Sam. We are figuring out this relationship thing as we go, one step at a time."

"You know you can come to me if you need to talk. About anything." Sam looked up from her task, and held Annie's gaze until she nodded. "Enough lecture for one day. Tell me, how are things coming with the plans for my wedding luncheon?"

The yellow flecks in Annie's brown eyes glimmered. "Heidi and I have almost nailed down the menu. Jackie is helping us with the decorations. You are gonna be so surprised."

"So Jackie's gotten involved, has she?" Sam said with a snicker.

"Um . . . maybe I wasn't supposed to say anything. I hope you're not mad if she helps."

"Of course I'm not mad. I just think it's funny. My sister can't help herself. She lives to plan parties."

Jackie's involvement explained why Heidi hadn't included a line item for decorations in her proposal. Sam received an estimate for the rentals—chairs, tables, and linens—and the expense of the food, including the seafood, which Sam was supplying through the market at cost. Heidi was providing all of the china, crystal, and flatware from her inventory for free.

"Just make sure Jackie doesn't go overboard like she tends to do."

"She's not," Annie said, shaking her head. "Simply elegant is her goal. She wanted me to ask you if you've done anything about flowers for the church."

"I've ordered several large white poinsettias. Tell her that's all I want."

"What about a bouquet?"

"I'm turning fifty in June, Annie. I don't need a bouquet." She quickly changed her mind when she saw the disappointed look on the girl's face. "Okay fine. Maybe something small."

Annie set her knife down and went to the sink to wash her hands. "I almost forgot. I have something to show you." She disappeared into the office and returned seconds later with a handful of drawings. "I know you don't want to send out invitations, but since you're having only a few guests, I thought something handmade might be special." She spread the drawings out on the counter.

Sam scraped her diced potatoes off the cutting board into a pot on the stove and turned her attention to the cards. "Did you make these yourself?"

Annie nodded.

Using watercolors, she had painted wreaths of greens with red berries on cream-colored card stock, and then created a calligraphed announcement of the nuptials between Sam and Eli with the date, time, and location of both the service and the reception beneath.

Sam ran her finger across the calligraphy. "They're really beautiful, Annie. I love them," she said, giving Annie a half hug. "You never cease to amaze me with your endless talents."

"I'm glad you like them. If you'll give me the list of your guests, Cooper and I will hand deliver them tomorrow."

Sam planted a kiss on the girl's cheek. "I couldn't love you more if you were my own daughter."

NINE

ON WEDNESDAY MORNING, Sam was on the phone helping Belinda Baker, one of her best customers, plan her Christmas brunch when Mimi Motte stormed into the market. She marched up to the counter and gestured at Sam to end her call. "I need to talk to you," she said in a loud whisper. "I don't have much time."

Jackie had worked for Mimi at Motte Interiors for fourteen years. Mimi had never been a fan of the Sweeney family, always acted as if the sisters and their mother were in some way inferior to her, but she'd been downright nasty toward them ever since Jackie resigned from her firm and took several of their key clients with her.

Sam turned her back on Mimi and stepped away from the counter while she concluded her call. "I know it's a difficult decision, Belinda. You want everything to be perfect for your family for Christmas. But you really can't go wrong with either the shrimp and grits or the crab casserole. Why don't you give it some thought and call me back once you've made your decision? We still have plenty of time."

Sam ended the call and jammed her cell phone in her back pocket. "Good grief, Mimi. What's the emergency? You act as if the sky is falling."

"This is worse! My caterer just walked out on me, and I have ten power couples coming for dinner tonight. My house is a wreck."

"At least you have oysters." Sam went to the kitchen and returned with the five dozen oysters Mimi had ordered. She set the netted bags on the counter and scanned the bar codes into the cash register.

Mimi jabbed her finger at the oysters. "And just who do you think is going to crack those? Did you not hear me, Samantha? I told you my caterer quit!" she said.

"I can't say I blame him if you yelled at him like that."

Mimi banged her fist on the counter. "You have to do something!"

"Calm down already." Sam cast a glance at the ship's clock over the door. "Robert is at lunch now. But if you leave the oysters with me, I'll have him crack them and display them on a tray of ice for you when he gets back."

"That only solves one of my many problems. I need a cook. I don't even know how to turn on the oven. And a florist. My arrangements always end up lopsided. This is a sit-down dinner for twenty-two. I need three servers minimum, two for the big table in the dining room and one for the smaller group I'm putting in the living room. Please, Samantha. You've got to help me." Mimi removed a tissue from her Louis Vuitton handbag and dabbed at her dry eyes.

Sam sighed. "I'm not sure what you want from me, Mimi.

I don't have a caterer in my back pocket." A thought occurred to her and she snapped her fingers. "On second thought, maybe I do. Heidi Butler, the woman who is planning my wedding luncheon, has just moved back to the East Coast from California. She's been doing a lot of work for Jackie's clients. I'm happy to call her to see if by any chance she's free."

Mimi sniffled. "Hmm. I don't know. I'm not in the habit of taking handouts from my competition."

"I'm offering you a referral for a caterer, Mimi. Not Jackie's client rejects. She's the only person I know who might be available. Take it or leave it."

Mimi slumped against the counter. "Fine. Call her."

Removing her cell phone from her pocket, she clicked on Heidi's contact information. When Heidi answered on the third ring, Sam explained the reason for her call.

"Let me see . . . If I juggle a few things around . . . I have two appointments this afternoon, but I can reschedule them for later in the week. I can get someone to cover for me at the Ravenel reception this evening. I think I can make it work. I'll be there in an hour."

Sam pressed the phone to her chest. "Heidi says she can be here in an hour."

Mimi snatched the phone away from Sam. "Mimi Motte here. I trust you can handle the flowers and the food. We'll need three servers as well."

Sam grabbed the phone back, set it on the counter, and pressed the speaker button. "You're on speaker now, Heidi." She glared across the counter at Mimi.

"I doubt I'll be able to find anyone on this short notice. Charleston is hopping with parties. Tis the season and all."

"That's not good enough. How can I possibly have a party without servers? I'll have to postpone."

"What about Annie?" Heidi suggested. "Can she help out?"

Mimi perked up. "Who's Annie?"

"My part-time help," Sam said. "She works here after school. She's a whiz in the kitchen. I can do without her for the afternoon."

"One down, two to go." Mimi shot Sam a quick head-to-toe glance. "What about you, Samantha? Are you free to work the party tonight?"

Sam hesitated. She'd rather have the dentist drill decay out of her tooth with no local anesthesia than spend the evening in Mimi's presence. On the other hand, Eli was working nights this week and she was growing tired of watching sappy Christmas movies on Lifetime. No sense in passing up an opportunity to earn a little extra money. Sam ran her fingers through her short hair. "Alright, fine. I can come over after we close the market at six."

"Two down—"

Sam held up her hand. "Take my advice, Mimi, and quit while you're ahead."

❆

Annie answered the door when Sam arrived at the Motte's sprawling contemporary house a few minutes past six.

"This house is amazing, Sam. Come see." She took Sam by the hand and dragged her through the downstairs. "Too bad you couldn't come during daylight. The view is amazing." Like a docent in a museum, she offered interesting tidbits as they passed through each room. "That grandfather clock in the corner belonged to Mimi's great-uncle. And the woman in the portrait above the fireplace was her grandmother, who once ate dinner with Queen Elizabeth. Can you believe that?" Photographs lined the hallway that led to the back of the house. "Look, there's George and Barbara Bush. Colin Powell. Condoleezza Rice." She leaned in close to Sam's ear. "The Mottes know everyone. There's Jack Nicklaus and that tennis player." Annie snapped her fingers. "I can't think of her name. She's way older than me."

"Chris Evert. Oh my word, is that . . ." Sam crossed the hall to get a better look. "It is! That's Mick Jagger." She scanned the photograph. "And Keith Richards." She took two steps farther down the hall. "And Jimmy Buffett. And Kenny Chesney. Holy cow! I had no idea the Mottes were so well connected." She lowered her voice. "We can't let Mimi hear us though. It'll go to her head."

Annie smiled. "Let me show you the dining room. Mimi has some beautiful pieces of silver." Sam followed Annie into the adjacent room that showcased the largest crystal chandelier and longest mahogany double pedestal table she'd ever seen. Annie pointed at the ornamental centerpiece on the table that displayed a stunning arrangement of red flowers—roses, calla lilies, and amaryllis. "Mimi calls that thing an epergne. Her husband bought it for her in an antique store in New York. I asked, and it's spelled e-p-e-r-g-n-e. Heidi let me help with the flowers. We soaked a block of oasis, which is like a green sponge, in water for twenty minutes. Then she stuck the flowers in the oasis."

Sam circled the table. "Everything looks lovely." She noticed the sideboard set with casserole dishes of all shapes and sizes. "And I see you solved the server problem by setting up a buffet."

"That was Heidi's idea." Mimi floated into the room on a cloud of flowery perfume so strong it took Sam's breath away. She was the picture of elegance in a green dress that clung to her toned figure. She ran her hand across the top of her gleaming silver chafing dish. "I haven't used some of these pieces in years. Annie did a marvelous job of polishing them." She pinched Sam's cheek so hard it hurt. "I owe you one. I will hire these two to cater all my parties from now on." After rearranging several of the serving utensils, Mimi moved on to inspect the rest of the room. She smoothed out a linen napkin at one place setting, and then adjusted a tulip that had begun to droop in the centerpiece. "Sam, please tell me you remembered to bring the oysters."

"They're in the back of my car. We'll leave them there until the party starts. It's so cold out, they'll be fine." Sam turned to Annie. "We should get to work. Can you show me the kitchen?"

They passed through the butler's pantry and entered an all-white kitchen with stainless steel appliances, marble countertops, and pickled pine floors. *And Mimi says she doesn't cook?*

Heidi stood at an island the size of Maui slicing new potatoes. Annie crossed the room to the oven. Grabbing a pair of pot holders, she removed the grits casserole, golden brown and bubbling, and set the Le Creuset dish on the stove. "Heidi had to remake the grits. The other caterer's were lumpy."

Sam raised a questioning eyebrow at Heidi who nodded. "I had to redo a lot of things. I don't know who the other caterer is, but his food is not up to my standards."

Sam dropped her coat and purse in the corner of the

kitchen. "No wonder Mimi fired him." She unwrapped a stick of butter and began slathering it on ham biscuits.

"Guess what, Sam." Annie removed two bunches of herbs from the sink and joined them at the island. "Heidi asked me to work for her this summer in Charleston."

Heidi looked up from her work. "Contingent upon your approval, of course. I've got several big parties and two weddings lined up." She gestured at Annie with her knife. "This one is a miracle worker."

Sam watched them as they worked. Annie was the right hand that instinctively knew how to aid the left. Heidi finished slicing potatoes, and then Annie scraped the contents of the cutting board onto a roasting pan. Annie sprinkled on rosemary and thyme while Heidi drizzled the potatoes with olive oil and balsamic vinegar. Heidi opened the door for Annie to slide in the pan.

"On to the salad," said Heidi as she stood back from the oven. They retrieved the salad ingredients from the enormous Sub-Zero refrigerator and returned to their cutting boards.

"I'm all for you working with Heidi this summer," Sam said. "It would be a great opportunity for you to learn since the food industry is obviously in your future. But I wouldn't want you driving home from Charleston alone late at night."

"I have an extra room," Heidi said. "She could stay with me."

Sam's interior radar sounded, alerting her to possible danger. This woman was a newcomer to their lives. What did they really know about Heidi? She could have some whacked-out sexual desire toward teenage girls. "That's kind of you to offer, but it probably makes more sense for her to stay at

Jackie's carriage house." Sam tore a sheet of aluminum foil off to cover the biscuits. "Have you ever been married, Heidi?"

"I was married once. A long time ago. Things didn't work out so well."

"Have you ever been tempted again? I'm sorry. I don't mean to pry."

"No worries." Heidi dismissed her with a wave of a cucumber. "My life is an open book. Truth is, I don't have the best judgment when it comes to men."

"Do you have any children?" Annie asked.

A faraway look settled on her face. "I had a baby when I was young. I was too selfish and immature and not ready to be a parent."

"Where is the baby now?" Annie asked.

Heidi set the cucumber on the cutting board and sliced it into thin slivers. "I gave her up for adoption."

TEN

THE DAYS FLEW off the December calendar as they raced toward Christmas. Sam put in long hours at work, helping her customers fulfill their holiday seafood needs, but she somehow managed to find time for tasks relating to the wedding. She took Eli to meet Pastor Paul, drove to Charleston for her final dress fitting, and sorted out the details of the pending sale of her Cape Cod and the purchase of the bungalow.

Late in the day on Friday, a week before Christmas, she was in the kitchen dicing potatoes when Jamie arrived with Sophia. The California girl was every bit as stunning as Jamie had described, with creamy skin, a thick mane of auburn hair, and blue eyes so cold and pale they reminded Sam of a glacier. Sam embraced her son, but when she made a move to hug Sophia, the girl thrust a limp hand out at her, as though daring her not to come too near.

Sam gripped Sophia's hand tight. "Welcome to our

home. You two must be starving. Eli has gone to the grocery for steaks."

Jamie's face lit up. "Can we cook them on the grill?"

Sam smiled. "That's the plan!"

Sophia rammed an elbow in Jamie's side. "We're going out to dinner, remember?" She batted her heavy eyelashes at Sam. "I hope you don't mind. Jamie promised to show me the town."

Her son's face fell. "Sorry, Mom. I forgot. I told Sophia I'd take her to the Pelican's Roost."

Sam bit back the sarcastic comments that flooded her mind. "That's fine. We'll save the steaks for tomorrow night." Sam returned her salad ingredients to the refrigerator. "I know you're disappointed not to spend the holiday with your folks, but how exciting for them to have the opportunity to go to Russia. Are they traveling with friends?"

"I'm not sure who they went with, now that you mention it. One of my father's clients, I think." Averting Sam's gaze, Sophia focused her attention on the strand of hair she was twirling around her finger.

The prickling of skin on the back of Sam's neck warned her that Sophia was not telling the truth. Why would she lie about such a thing? Was her family life at home that unhappy?

"In any case, we're happy to have you here with us. Why don't I show you your room?" With Jamie wheeling her suitcase behind them, Sam led Sophia down the hall to the guest room. "I put clean towels in the bathroom next door. I hope you don't mind sharing it with me."

"How quaint. It'll be just like at the sorority house."

Sam considered snatching the girl's pert nose off her face,

but she excused herself instead. "I'll leave you to get settled. Let me know if you need anything."

Jamie followed her back to the kitchen. He went straight to the refrigerator, removed a container of tuna salad, and began shoveling it in his mouth with a fork. "This is really good. Did you change the recipe?"

"Annie tweaked it a bit. You'll have to ask her what she added."

He ate half the container before replacing the lid. "I can't believe you're getting married in a week. Are you excited?"

"We've been so busy at the market, I haven't had much time to think about it." Sam lifted the cutting board and scraped the potato skins down the disposal.

"About the market. Do you think you can manage without me? I can't just leave Sophia to entertain herself."

"I agree. That would be rude," Sam said, rinsing the cutting board. "We'll manage without you."

Jamie plopped down on the nearest bar stool. "Can we put the tree up on Sunday?"

"I've been meaning to talk to you about that." She set the cutting board in the drying rack and turned around to face him. "I've been thinking that maybe we won't have a tree this year. It's one less thing we have to worry about with the move."

"Are you kidding me? It's Christmas. We can't just not have a tree."

Sophia entered the room and sat down next to Jamie, sliding her bar stool closer to his. "I'm with your mom on this. Christmas trees are such a hassle. We have a staff that takes care of ours."

"How sad for you. Some of my happiest memories of

Christmases past are of our tree-decorating parties." Sam rubbed her temples, feeling the onset of a headache. "Why don't we compromise, Jamie, and put up a small tree this year?"

"Deal. Sophia and I will pick up a small tree tomorrow, and bring the ornaments down from the attic. We'll decorate it on Sunday. Can we have a pizza party?"

Eli came through the back door with a grocery bag in each hand. "What's this about pizza? I thought we were having steaks."

"We're talking about Sunday when we decorate the tree," Jamie said. "Do you want to help?"

"Of course." He set his bags down on the counter and introduced himself to Sophia. He pecked Sam on the cheek. "I'm glad you decided to get a tree. I think you'll be glad you did."

She leaned into him. "You won't be so glad after Christmas when we have to deal with a dead tree while packing up to move."

Eli massaged her shoulders. "I have a solution for that. We'll drag the whole thing, ornaments and lights, to the curb."

"Oh no you won't! Not with *my* ornaments." She had every ornament Jamie had ever made in school. Once he got old enough, he saved money from his allowance every year to buy her a special ornament relating to something that had happened during the past twelve months. The year she'd taken him to Disney World and he'd snuck off to the gift shop and purchased a glass ball with Mickey Mouse ears and 2005 painted on it had been a longtime favorite.

Sophia nudged Jamie. "Is this move happening soon? I'm pretty sure you forgot to mention that little detail to me."

"We have to be out of this house by the twenty-eighth," Sam explained. "We assumed you'd be leaving after Christmas to visit other friends or family members."

Sophia shook her head. "Jamie invited me to come home with him for the break, which isn't over until mid-January." She jutted out her chin. "Oh well. There's nothing we can do about it now. I promise not to get in your way."

An awkward silence filled the room.

What did Jamie see in this girl? This sorority diva. So-Diva. Sam mentally smacked herself. *Give her a chance, Sam. She may surprise you.*

Sophia slid off the bar stool and pulled Jamie with her. "We should probably get going. I don't know about you, but I'm starving."

Eli waited for the young couple to leave before he turned to Sam. "I thought we were cooking steaks."

"Sophia insisted Jamie take her out to dinner," Sam said as she opened and closed cabinet doors.

"What're you looking for?" Eli asked.

She slumped back against the counter. "Something that isn't here. Why is it that I always want a drink the minute something bad happens or someone rubs me the wrong way?"

Eli took her in his arms. "Because you've only been sober for a hundred and eighty-five days."

"This time. Last time I went eleven months before I lapsed."

"It gets easier. I promise." He nipped at her earlobe. "We need to do something to take your mind off of—"

"SoDiva—the blood-sucking she-devil who has my son wrapped around her finger?" Sam planted her face in his chest. "What're we going to do about her?"

"Nothing. Jamie will figure this out for himself." Eli kissed the top of her head. "I admit she came on a bit strong. Maybe she's just nervous about meeting her boyfriend's family for the first time. Let's give her a chance. Jamie is a good kid. If he sees something in her, there must be something to see."

"That's what my good inner self keeps telling me. My bad inner self isn't being nearly as kind or understanding."

Eli laughed. "You need a break," he said, holding her at arm's length. "You've been working too hard. It's warm outside. Why don't we go for a walk down on the docks and grab a bite to eat?"

Sam smiled. "That sounds nice. Anywhere but the Pelican's Roost."

The brisk evening air along the waterfront cleared their heads and increased their appetites. Instead of going out to dinner, they picked up burgers and a salad from the Main Street Grill and returned home. With the gas fire keeping them warm and cozy, they ate in front of the television, watching *The Holiday* with Cameron Diaz for what seemed like the millionth time. Eli said goodnight a few minutes past eleven.

Sam had never needed to set a curfew for Jamie. He'd never been one to stay out late. But when the clock struck one and there was no sign of Jamie and Sophia, she sent several urgent texts to him. He didn't respond. She paced in front of the sitting-room window with one eye on the lookout for headlights in the driveway. When her legs began to ache, she reminded herself that her son was a college student and that he probably stayed out much later at school. She forced herself to go back to bed. Forty-five minutes later, she was still wide awake and staring at the ceiling when the back door slammed. At the sound of giggling in the hallway, she cracked her bedroom door and peeked outside. Jamie had Sophia pinned against the wall, her long legs wrapped around his waist.

Sam cleared her throat. "I've been worried sick about the two of you. Time to go to bed. I have to get up early for work in the morning."

She closed the door without waiting for a response. Muffled laughter echoed throughout the hallway for several seconds before they finally grew silent. Sam went to the kitchen for a cup of Sleepytime tea. She was already stretched thin. The last thing she needed was a house full of inconsiderate teenagers keeping her up all night.

ELEVEN

S AM SPENT THE day on Saturday directing her staff and filling orders for customers with last-minute seafood needs. Annie peeled shrimp until her fingers bled. Cooper and Sean returned to the inlet three times for oysters. And Lovie recited recipes for everything from sautéed scallops to she crab soup. No one complained, especially not Sam. The booming business guaranteed her staff a healthy Christmas bonus, and the surplus would carry them through the slow winter months ahead.

Sam checked her cell phone frequently for texts from Jamie and kept an eye on the front door hoping he might stop by to show Sophia the shop. When four o'clock came and went with no word from him, she began to worry. Jamie never went for long periods of time without checking in with her. At least not while he was in town. She arrived home a few minutes after six to find the pickup Jamie had purchased with the money he'd earned over the summer was not in the driveway. Nor was there a Christmas tree resting against the side of the house in a bucket of water. Sam felt the itch to wrap her fingers around the neck of a bottle of booze, but she brewed a cup of peppermint tea instead. She was sitting at the island, sipping on lukewarm tea, when Jamie and Sophia arrived around seven, loaded down with shopping bags.

"I take it you've been shopping?" Sam asked.

"We went to Charleston." Sophia dropped her bags in the middle of the floor. "The shopping is subpar, but I managed to find a few things."

Jamie leaned over Sam's shoulder and pecked her cheek. "I bought something for you."

"What, a Christmas ornament to hang on the tree you forgot to buy?" Sam cringed at the sarcastic tone in her voice. She'd promised herself she'd remain cool.

Jamie took a step back. "Ouch! Hostile," he said, rubbing his arm. "For your information, the tree is in the back of my truck. It meets your criteria—fat and full and short like me."

"Five eight is not short. At least not according to Eli." She stood to face her son, and cupped his chin "I'm sorry I snapped at you."

His dark eyes brightened. "You're forgiven."

"Did you put the tree in water?"

"No, but I will before we go out."

Sam removed her hand from his face. "Where are you going? I thought we were cooking the steaks tonight?"

He shot an uncertain look at Sophia. "I was going to talk to you about that. Rachel, one of Sophia's sorority sisters who lives in town, has invited some people over."

"The steaks will keep another night, won't they?" Sophia nodded a yes before Sam had a chance to consider the question.

Sam let out a deep breath. "That actually works better for Eli and me. We're supposed to stop in at Brad's." Eli's partner and his wife, Judy, had invited some of the guys on the police force and their wives over for an impromptu get-together. "Tell me, does this Rachel have a last name?"

"Bennett," Jamie said. "But I doubt you know her. She wasn't in my graduating class at PHS. She went off to boarding school in Virginia."

"You're not talking about Donna Bennett's daughter, are you?" Sam shared a mutual dislike with Donna that traced back to childhood.

"I have no idea." Jamie nudged Sophia. "Is her mom's name Donna?"

"How would I know?" Sophia snapped.

"It must be the same Bennett. This town is only so big. I'm warning you, Jamie," Sam said with a jabbing finger. "Mind your manners while you're in their home."

"Geez, Mom. I'm not going on a playdate. Stop treating me like a baby."

Sam's face tightened. "You are still my child as long as you're living under my roof and I'm paying your tuition. And not so late tonight, son. We have church in the morning."

Jamie's jaw dropped. "Come on, Mom. Cut me some slack. I'm in college. I don't have a curfew when I'm at school."

"Well you do while you're at home."

"No one's stopping you from going to bed, Mom."

"Going to bed and sleeping are two different things. I can't rest easy until I know you're home safe and sound, especially since you have a houseguest."

"We'll be quiet tonight, Sam. I promise." Sophia took

Jamie by the hand and dragged him across the kitchen. "We better get changed. Rachel is expecting us soon."

Sam watched them go. *Sam? I don't remember giving her permission to call me by my first name.*

She was still sitting at the island, pondering this younger generation, wondering how they'd become so rude and entitled, when Jamie and Sophia left around seven thirty. "Don't forget to put the tree in water," she called after them.

"I'm on it," Jamie said, a fraction of a second before Sophia slammed the door shut.

When Eli arrived a few minutes later, he found her staring into her empty teacup. "Tough day?" he asked, sliding onto the bar stool beside her.

"Yes and no." She leaned back in her chair. "Business is great. No complaints there. But I'm exhausted. Jamie and Sophia stayed out way too late last night. What's wrong with me that I can't go to sleep until he gets home? I'm sure other parents with kids in college don't wait up for them."

"I wouldn't know. Obviously. But I imagine I would feel the same in your shoes. Not only are you concerned for Jamie, you're responsible for his houseguest as well." He tilted her head back and kissed her lips. "Are you up for going to Brad's? I get the impression the guys are planning a surprise for us."

Sam's eyes widened. "You mean like a wedding shower?"

He traced her lips with his finger. "I could be wrong. No one has mentioned anything specific, but a lot of whispering has gone on behind my back at the station lately."

Sam had a sudden sinking feeling. "You don't think they're planning to take you off for a wild night of bachelor partying somewhere, do you?"

"And risk the wrath of Samantha Sweeney? I don't think so."

"I wouldn't be too sure. If they try to kidnap you, they'll have to do so over my dead body." She hopped off the bar stool. "Who knows? Maybe going to Brad and Judy's will help take my mind off SoDiva. But you'll have to drive. I'm low on gas."

She pulled him to his feet, and he leaned in to kiss her neck. "Pee-yew. You smell like fish. I'll put your Christmas tree in water while you go shower."

She pushed him away. "Jamie was supposed to do that."

"He must have forgotten." Eli dipped his head toward the backyard. "Because it's lying in the grass beside the garage."

Sam flushed. "He's the one who wanted that damn tree. I swear, I don't know what's gotten into him. He usually does what I ask, and without me having to ask a second time."

"Don't be too hard on him, honey. He's distracted. His girl is in town. It's Christmastime and they're in love."

Sam's head shot up. "In love? Please god, no! That girl is definitely not what I have in mind for my son."

❋

Judy Swanson was Sam's favorite of all the policemen's wives. She was tiny, barely five feet tall, with a cap of unruly silver curls that sprang from her head like Slinkys. She greeted them at the door with a couple of nonalcoholic beers. "We know how much the two of you hate being the center of attention. And you would never have agreed to a party if we'd asked. So we planned a surprise shower for you instead." She led Eli and Sam to the game room on the first floor of their split-level ranch where Eli's coworkers and their wives stood chatting around a pile of gifts. "We thought an around-the-clock shower, where everyone brings a gift for entertaining at a particular time of day or night, might give the two of you the hint." Judy clapped her hands. "Invite us to the bungalow. Soon."

Much to her surprise, Sam enjoyed opening their presents, receiving gifts that she and Eli would share as husband and wife. They got one of everything anyone would ever need to throw a party—trays, platters, serving utensils, salad tongs, insulated tumblers, crystal glasses. Someone even gave them a waffle iron.

"This is too much," Sam said, spreading her arms wide when the last gift had been opened. "I can hardly wait to invite you all to our new home as soon as we get settled."

Brad stepped forward. "We have one last gift." He turned to Sam. "I'm sorry. It's more for Eli, but you'll benefit from it in a different way." He opened the back door to the patio. "Unfortunately you're gonna have to come outside in the cold to receive it."

The party guests filed out and gathered around a large green oval-shaped contraption.

"What is that?" Sam asked.

"It's a Big Green Egg, only the best charcoal grill-slash-smoker money can buy," Eli said, running his hand over the ceramic surface of the grill. "I can't believe you bought this for me."

Brad slapped Eli on the back. "We wanted to do something special for you. This seemed like the obvious choice, since you're the official grill master."

Eli lifted the lid. "You guys shouldn't have. I know how much these things cost."

"Evan Brewster over at the hardware store was more than

happy to cut us a deal when he found out we were buying it for you." Brad peered inside the cooking chamber. "I'll keep it for you until you get settled in your new house. I thought I'd christen it on Christmas Eve with my beef tenderloin."

Eli laughed. "You go right ahead."

Brad turned to his gas grill behind him. "In the meantime, we need to fire this baby up if we want to eat before midnight."

The men cooked hamburgers while the women arranged the assortment of salads and side dishes they'd all contributed on the dining room table. They went back to the game room to eat where the discussion quickly turned to police work. The men entertained their wives with stories of courage and funny tales of life as small-town cops.

Eli and Sam were loading their gifts in the back of the police cruiser when he received a call from Luke Tanner, a rookie member of the force who was working the night shift. Eli listened for a minute before he said, "I'm on my way," and hung up.

"What's wrong?" Sam asked.

"Luke busted a party at a house on Creekside out past Moss Creek Farm. A bunch of underage kids drinking, mostly college students."

"Let me guess. Jamie is one of them."

"And Sophia." Eli slammed the trunk closed. "We need to get out there." They climbed in the car and Eli peeled out down the street.

"What are the penalties for a minor in possession charge?" Sam asked, gripping the handle on the roof when Eli made a sudden sharp turn.

"If Luke writes him a ticket, Jamie would have to

pay a small fine and attend an alcohol prevention education program."

"That might not be all bad. Maybe he'll learn a thing or two."

Eli approached a red light and looked both ways before cruising on through. "According to Luke, there are at least fifty kids out here. He has a crew on site and they're breathalyzing all of them."

"Including Jamie?"

"He didn't say. All I know is, he's holding Jamie and Sophia in the back of his squad car out in front of the house."

"Where are the parents? I know the mother, you know. Donna Bennett may be my least favorite person in the whole world."

"Out of town, apparently."

Upon arrival at the scene, Eli pulled up beside the other patrol cars parked haphazardly in the driveway. Sam started to get out of the car, but Eli grabbed her arm. "I think it's better if you let me handle this. I'm hoping I can convince Luke to release them into my custody without writing them a ticket."

"You're in charge." Sam settled back in her seat. "As far as I'm concerned, he can throw the two of them in jail. Tell him to keep them there until after Christmas. At least they'll stay safe and out of trouble."

TWELVE

SAM HAD NEVER seen her son drunk before. She'd known him to have an occasional beer at a tailgate party, or a family event like Faith's wedding. It's not that she was naive. She suspected he drank in excess on occasion at school. He'd just never done it around her. Perhaps out of respect for her addiction problems. Now, with slurred speech and bloodshot eyes, he was more than a little tipsy. And Sophia was totally in the bag. Her head dangled from her neck, lolling back and forth every time the car turned.

"I'm not sure how I feel about Luke letting the two of you off the hook." Sam leaned in between the seats so she could see Sophia and Jamie in the back. "I don't need to tell you how disappointed I am. Especially in you, Jamie. You know how hard I struggle with my addiction. You realize that certain aspects of alcoholism are inherited."

"Ah, Mom." Jamie swatted his hand at her. "I'm not an alcoholic. I hardly ever drink. It's just tonight . . . well, I had a teensy-weensy hit off Rachel's brother's bong."

Sophia's body stiffened and her head shot up. "Don't tell your mother that, you idiot." She shoved Jamie, and he toppled over, breaking into a fit of laughter.

"Drinking is one thing, Jamie," Sam said, when he finally stopped laughing. "But I won't tolerate drug use of any kind."

Jamie smacked the back of Sam's seat. "Haven't you heard, Mom? It's legal to smoke weed in this country."

Eli sought Jamie out in the rearview mirror. "Not in the country, son. Only four states have legalized marijuana for recreational use, one of which is definitely not South Carolina. But I'm pretty sure you know this already."

"Yes, sir," Jamie said, his brow knitted.

"Don't worry, honey," Eli said to Sam. "The drug dogs are searching the Bennett's house now. They'll find whatever's left and destroy it."

"Of all people, you had to pick Donna Bennett's daughter to party with. That woman will smear your name all over town whether you're guilty or not. I can't believe—"

Eli cut Sam off with a shake of his head. "You're wasting your breath, sweetheart," he said, his voice not much more than a whisper. "Save the lecture for when he's sober."

She shifted in her seat to face the front. "You're right. I doubt he even remembers any of this in the morning." She propped her cowboy boots on the dash and buried her face in her hands for the rest of the ride home.

Eli parked on the curb in front of the house. "It's been a long night. I suggest we all go to bed, and talk about this in the morning."

"After church," Sam added.

Jamie hiccuped. "Yeah! After you calm down."

"I can't get out." Sophia said, struggling with the door handle. "What's wrong with this stupid door?"

Eli clicked the unlock button. "Sorry. I had you locked in."

"I don't feel so good." With one hand covering her mouth, Sophia pushed the door open and ran toward the house. She was halfway to the front porch when she stopped in her tracks, bent over, and projectile vomited all over the sidewalk.

Sam, Jamie, and Eli jumped out of the car and rushed to her side.

"That's gross," Jamie said, staring down at the throw up. "I see chunks of pizza in there."

Eli gripped Jamie's shoulder. "This is serious, son. We may need to take her to the hospital. Do you know what and how much she had to drink or smoke tonight?"

Jamie looked up from the vomit and took a step back. "No, sir. She was hanging out with her friends most of the time. They played beer pong for a while at the kitchen table."

"So she was only drinking beer?"

Jamie screwed his face up as he thought about it. "Now that I think about it. One of them had a bottle of tequila. I don't know if she drank any."

"Did she smoke any marijuana?" Sam asked.

"I have no idea."

Sophia dropped to her knees and threw up again. "Let's get her inside." Eli swept her into his arms and carried her to the house.

Jamie started off behind Eli, but Sam grabbed him by the arm. "Not so fast." She pointed at the vomit on the sidewalk. "Get the hose and wash this mess off. That's the last thing I want to see tomorrow morning when I come out for the paper."

"But, Mom!" Jamie wrapped his arms around his chest. "It's freezing out here."

Sam realized for the first time that her son wasn't wearing his coat. "Good. That means you'll get the job done quicker." She turned her back on him and headed up the sidewalk. "By the way, you're in double the trouble if you lost your new coat," she called over her shoulder.

Sam found Eli in the bathroom holding Sophia's thick auburn hair back from her face while she puked in the toilet.

He looked up at Sam. "Do you have any idea where this girl's parents are?"

"In Moscow. That's all I know." Sam handed him a washcloth to wipe Sophia's mouth.

"She's probably fine, but since we're responsible for her in her parents' absence, just to be on the safe side, I think we should call Mike."

"Good idea. I'll see if I can get him on the phone." Sam went into the hall where her voice wouldn't echo. Her brother-in-law answered on the second ring. "I'm sorry to bother you so late, Mike, but I have an emergency and I need your advice." She explained the situation.

"Vomiting is a good sign, but I'm happy to check her out anyway."

"I'll bring her in right away. Will you be at the hospital for a while?"

"Actually, I'm at home. I have the night off. Why don't I come to you?"

"I hate to ask you to do that." She heard Sophia retching in the bathroom and quickly added, "But under the circumstances, I'll take you up on the offer."

Mike arrived fifteen minutes later with his cheeks pink from the cold and his hair disheveled. "I spoke to Jamie on the way in. I think he's afraid to come inside."

"He should be," Sam said.

Mike snickered. "I grilled him a little. Aside from being slightly intoxicated, he seems fine."

"Trust me, he won't be tomorrow when I'm finished with him."

Mike patted Sam on the shoulder. "Even good kids make mistakes sometimes."

"My good kid appears to be under the spell of an extraordinarily selfish, inconsiderate young woman."

He shrugged off his coat and dropped it in the chair beside the door. "Is this selfish and inconsiderate young woman Sophia? The girl Jamie is gaga over?"

"The one and only. Come meet her for yourself." Sam led him to the bathroom.

Mike inclined his head in greeting to Eli and bent down beside Sophia on the floor. "How much has she vomited?" he asked as he felt her pulse.

"Outside twice, and four times in here," Eli said. "I doubt there's much left in her stomach."

"Is she making any sense?"

"She was talking some gibberish. But she seems to know where she is and that her parents are spending the holidays in Russia."

"Let's see if we can get her to sit up." Together they helped Sophia to a sitting position. Mike tapped her lightly on the cheek. "Sophia, can you hear me?"

She cracked an eyelid and a bloodshot blue eye appeared. "Who are you?"

"I'm Jamie's uncle, Mike. I'm also an ER doctor. I think you should go to the emergency room and get some IV fluids. You'll be glad you did in the morning."

"No! I'm not going to any hospital." Sophia wiped spittle from her mouth with her sleeve. "I'll be fine. I just need two Advil and a tall glass of water." Using the toilet for support, she hauled herself to her feet. She took two steps, stumbled, righted herself, and then wobbled out of the bathroom.

Sam shook her head in wonder at the girl's rapid recovery. "Two Advil and a tall glass of water? Sounds like she's been in this condition before."

They moved to the hallway. "She'll be fine," Mike said. "But you should keep an eye on her tonight. If you have any concerns, take her to the emergency room." He handed Sam a business card. "I've written the name of the attending physician on the back, along with his cell number. I spoke to him on the way over here. Several other kids from this same party were brought in in similar condition."

"Why do these kids drink themselves into such a state?" Sam asked. "Speaking from my own experience, I understand all too well why adults abuse alcohol, but what sorrows do these kids have to drown?"

"You'd be surprised at the challenges facing our nation's youth," Mike said. "The peer pressure brought on by social media alone is enough to destroy their confidence. They struggle with their identities. Competition to get into good colleges is at an all-time high. They come from divided homes. Pressure to perform on the sporting fields is out of control. And the drinking age doesn't help. They're going to drink, regardless of the law. But they aren't allowed to drink in public, so they're forced to hide it, which means they end up abusing alcohol by drinking too much, too quick." He gave Sam's shoulder a pat. "You're lucky you haven't faced any of these issues with Jamie. He's a great kid. You've done a good job. Go easy on him."

Jamie was waiting for them inside the front door. "I'm sorry you had to come over, Uncle Mike. This shouldn't have happened."

"You're right. It shouldn't have happened. But it did. Learn from your mistakes." Mike slapped Jamie on the back. "Be good to your mom. She's getting married in a few days. She needs her beauty rest."

Sam hugged Mike goodbye. "It's nice to have a doctor in the family. I owe you one."

"I'm glad to be of help." He slipped on his coat and hurried down the sidewalk to his car.

Jamie draped his arm over Sam's shoulder. "Mom, I'm—"

She pushed him away. "Not tonight, Jamie. I'm too tired. We will talk about this tomorrow. After I've calmed down and you have sobered up.

Jamie looked to Eli for help, but Eli shot back, "Go to bed, son."

"Yes, sir." Shoulders slumped, he plodded off toward his room.

Sam called after him, "And I expect you to be up and dressed for church no later than ten thirty." She fell back against the door. "What a night! One the most pleasant evenings I've spent in a long time turned into the worst. We still need to unload all our gifts."

"Let's just leave them in the car, and I'll take them to the new house on Monday after we close."

She wrapped her arms around his waist, hugging him tight. "Thank you for tonight, for all you did for Jamie. I don't know what I'd do without you, Lt. Marshall."

"I'm going to do my best to make sure you never find out."

THIRTEEN

ELI SPENT THE night on the sofa in order to keep an ear out for Sophia so Sam could get the sleep she needed. Around eight the next morning, he went home to shower and change for church. Everyone made roll call except Sophia who was snoring like a sailor when they left.

"Mom, about last night," Jamie started as Eli was backing the Jeep out of the driveway. He'd taken Sam's car home when he went to change and filled it up with gasoline on the way back.

"Not now, Jamie. We'll talk about it after church." Sam needed time to think about what words of wisdom she wanted to impart to her son.

Reverend Webster delivered a poignant sermon about the power of forgiveness, especially during the holidays.

Is he speaking directly to me? she wondered. *Does he somehow know about last night's incident with Jamie?*

As was their custom, Sam met with the rest of her family on the sidewalk in front of the church after the service. She gave Mike a hug and whispered yet another thank you in his ear. "Jamie's embarrassed about last night, as he should be."

"Don't worry," Mike said. "No one will hear about it from me. I don't even think Faith knows I left the house last night."

"I don't mind if Faith knows. I'll tell her myself. But, for Jamie's sake, I'd rather Mom not find out about this."

Lovie had offered to take all of them to lunch, but everyone had begged off, claiming holiday preparations that needed attention.

"Where is she, Jamie?" Lovie searched the throng of churchgoers exiting the sanctuary. "I'm dying to meet your girl."

"I'm sorry, Gran. She's not here. Sophia is Catholic. It's against her religion to attend a Protestant church."

"Oh. I see." Lovie's eyes fell from the crowd to her grandson.

"You'll meet her this week. I promise. Maybe I'll bring her by the market."

Lovie forced a smile on her face. "Be sure that you do."

The family bid their goodbyes and took off in opposite directions.

Sam dragged Jamie to the car by the collar of his blue blazer. "It's not enough for you to smoke pot and bring your girlfriend home so drunk I had to call your uncle to come over in the middle of the night to check her out. Now you have to lie to your grandmother? What's gotten into you?"

"It wasn't really a lie, Mom. Sophia told me she wasn't comfortable going to our church. Last night was bad. I'm really sorry. I promise nothing like that will ever happen again."

She opened the car door and pointed at the backseat. "Get in." She climbed into the car behind him. "You've been responsible about your drinking until now. At least when you're at home. For all I know, last night's behavior might be the norm for you when you're at school. I'd like to think you've learned something from watching me struggle with my addiction. But I will not tolerate the drug use."

"Trust me, Mom. I get it. I totally screwed up. I told you that Coach randomly drug tests us during the season. I'm sure it won't take long for the little bit of pot I smoked last night to leave my system. But it was a dumb move. I don't want to do anything to risk my scholarship or my chances of starting next year."

Eli started the car and turned on the heat. "You put your mom in a bad predicament last night, Jamie. Sophia's parents are out of the country, on the other side of the world. They left their daughter in your care, which means our care. If anything bad had happened . . ."

Jamie hung his head. "I know. I'll talk to her."

"I suggest you do," Sam said. "Because I don't need any more drama, especially not this week when things are already so hectic."

"I didn't really think it through when Sophia invited herself for Christmas."

Sam locked eyes with Eli. *Invited herself?*

Eli gave a slight shake of his head, warning her that now was not the appropriate time to bring it up.

Jamie went on, "I know how busy you are at the market. I want to help you. I really do. But I can't just leave Sophia at our house all day alone. I could bring her to work with me, but I'm not sure she's cut out for peddling seafood."

"You're right about that." Sam didn't want SoDiva anywhere near her place of business.

"I can't just sit around all day and do nothing," Jamie said. "Is there something I can do to help you around the house? I can start packing for the move."

Sam tossed her hands up. "Finally! You are beginning to sound like my son."

Eli put the car in gear and they headed toward home.

"I have boxes and packing paper in the garage," Sam said. "Pack the kitchen first. I bought paper plates for us to use this week, but leave out some eating utensils."

❋

Eli dropped Sam at home, and then took Jamie to pick up his truck at last night's party scene. She prepared a brunch of scrambled eggs, sausage, and biscuits while they were gone. No matter how many cabinet doors she slammed and pots she banged around, she could not rouse Sophia from sleep.

"Do you think Sophia will ever come out of her room?" Sam asked over coffee.

Jamie shrugged. "She'll come out when she gets hungry."

"She's probably afraid to face you," Eli said.

"Ha. I don't think Sophia is afraid of anything," said Sam.

When Eli left to tend to his own chores, Jamie went to the attic for the tree ornaments and Sam retired to her bedroom to wrap the pile of gifts stuffed under her bed. Around two o'clock, she heard the bathroom door click shut and the shower turn on.

Princess SoDiva has emerged from her castle.

An hour later, Sam found Sophia curled up on the sofa watching something on her iPad, a half-eaten pimento cheese sandwich and a sweating glass of iced tea on the table next to her.

Sam picked up the glass and used her shirttail to wipe the condensation from the table. "I'll get the jar of mayonnaise for you to rub that out."

Sophia followed her gaze to the watermark. "Oops."

Sam's nostrils flared. "We missed you at church this morning. My family was looking forward to meeting you."

Sophia returned her attention to her iPad. "My family doesn't go to church."

"How sad for you." Sam took three steps toward the kitchen and turned back around. "What you do in your own home doesn't concern me, but last night's behavior will not be tolerated in mine. If it happens again, I'll be forced to call your parents."

Sophia's eyes remained glued to the iPad. "Really, Sam? We're not in middle school anymore. But have fun trying to reach them in Russia."

Sam spun around and stomped off to the kitchen. This insolent little bitch would get what was coming to her eventually.

For the rest of the day, Sophia didn't move from her spot on the sofa. Even when Jamie and Sam wrestled the Christmas tree into the room. Even when Sam handed Jamie a list and sent him off to the store. Even when Sam set the table for dinner in the adjoining dining room. Even when Jamie asked if she wanted to go outside with him to grill.

"My patience is growing thin," Sam said to Eli when he brought in the steaks.

"I know, baby. But trust me, none of this spoiled brat behavior is lost on Jamie."

They gathered around the ancient walnut table in the dining room and Eli offered the blessing. Sam took in the floral wallpaper that was outdated ten years ago. "Sad to think that this will be our last meal in this dining room. At this table for that matter, if my sister has anything to do with it."

Sophia brightened. "Then we should celebrate with some wine."

Eli raised an eyebrow. " A little hair of the dog?"

Sophia's lip curled up in a snarl. "What. Ever. We always have wine with dinner at my house."

"You're a guest in someone else's home," Eli said. "As the saying goes, when in Rome . . ."

"Eli and I are alcoholics," Sam said. "I don't keep booze in the house."

A gloomy silence settled over the table. Sam usually had much to share with Jamie and Eli at Sunday dinner when they planned their week. With business booming at the market and the wedding in six days, there was plenty to discuss. But Sophia's sulky presence put a damper on their holiday spirit. She picked at her food, barely taking more than a bite of her steak.

"Are you a vegetarian?" Sam asked, eyeing her untouched meat.

Sophia pushed her plate away and got up. "I don't have much of an appetite. If you'll excuse me." She left the room and her untouched plate on the table.

Sam glanced down at the plate and then up at her son. "Obviously her *staff* at home does more for Sophia's family than decorate their Christmas tree."

Jamie snatched up both his and Sophia's plates and walked them to the kitchen. Sam heard the water running as he rinsed the plates. "Thanks for dinner," he said as he passed through the dining room on his way to join his girlfriend on the sofa.

Eli reached for her hand. "I'm sorry, honey. I don't even know what to say."

"Neither do I." She gulped in a lungful of air. "We can't let SoDiva spoil our holiday. Especially not this year when we have so much to celebrate. After we finish with the dishes, we're going to march in there,"—she pointed at the doorway leading to the sitting room—"turn on some Christmas music, and decorate our tree in true Sweeney style."

"That's my girl."

Jamie had already started putting the lights on the tree by the time Sam and Eli joined them. Sam connected her iPhone to her speaker and accessed her Christmas music playlist on iTunes. She turned to face Eli and Jamie. "I'm excited about our new house. But tonight I want to celebrate all the wonderful times we've had here." She raised her arms in the air. "Let the decorating begin!"

Sophia on the sofa forgotten, the threesome spent the next two hours bedecking the tree. They scaled back on the number of ornaments and lights that they usually used, but the process went a long way to improving their moods.

"Here, you do the honors." Sam handed Jamie the angel topper when they were nearing completion. "I'm glad you insisted we put up a tree for our last Christmas."

As he situated the angel on top of the tree, Jamie said, "Everything doesn't have to change, you know. You're getting married and we're moving, but we still have our traditions."

Eli ripped open a package of tinsel. "And I'm excited to share in those traditions."

Sam grabbed a handful of tinsel and tossed it on the tree. "And we can start new ones that include you."

"I agree, Mom. Next year we should mix it up, do things a little different."

"What did you have in mind?" she asked.

"An oyster roast. We can invite all our friends, yours and mine. Make it an annual thing."

She smiled. "No mystery about who's going to supply the oysters."

Jamie and Eli draped tinsel from the top branches above Sam's head, and they stood back to admire their handiwork. Eli hooked his arm around Sam's waist. "This time tomorrow, we'll be the proud owners of waterfront property."

"So tomorrow is big day number one," Jamie said, the lights from the tree reflected in his dark eyes. "What time is the closing?"

"Four o'clock," Eli said. "If all goes as planned with the bank."

"We should celebrate," Jamie said. "Why don't we take dinner over to the new house tomorrow and hang out?"

"I'm working nights until Wednesday," Eli said. "But we'll do plenty of celebrating this weekend."

"Did somebody mention a party?" Setting her iPad aside, Sophia stood and stretched. She walked over to the tree and inspected if from different angles. "Tinsel is kinda tacky, don't you think?"

"That's why we like it," Sam and Jamie said in unison.

Like a cat slinking across the room, Sophia moved to the window and peeked through the blinds. "I'm bored. Isn't there anything to do in this town?"

Jamie shook his head. "I tried to warn you, Soph. Prospect is not a happening place."

"Then we'll have to make our own fun. Lucky for you, I'm tired tonight." She retrieved her iPad from the sofa before heading off to bed.

FOURTEEN

EVERYTHING THAT POSSIBLY could go wrong did go wrong at the market on Monday morning. One of the larger coolers had stopped working over the weekend, resulting in several hundred dollars worth of lost merchandise. Their weekly shipment of fish failed Sam's sniff test, and a cement mixer rear-ended the wine distributor on his way into town from Charleston, transforming the highway into a river of red wine.

Sam was in the back office, leaving her third message for the refrigerator repairman, when Faith arrived around nine. "Mike told me about Sophia. He said you wouldn't mind me knowing. It sounds like you've got your hands full. Is there anything I can do to help?"

"We've got it under control, but thank you." Sam opened the desk drawer and shook two tablets out of the bottle of Advil. "I keep hoping Sophia will show some redeeming qualities, but that's looking less and less likely with each passing day."

"Jamie needs to see this side of her for himself if this is in fact the true Sophia."

"That's what Eli keeps telling me."

"You realize that the best way to get a girlfriend to show her true colors is to take her home to meet your parents. That goes for boyfriends too of course."

Sam thought about Eli and how thoughtful and considerate he was to her mother. "That's very true. Let's just hope something good will come from her bad behavior."

During a lull in business later that morning, Sam asked Annie if she'd met Sophia.

"Briefly. Jamie introduced me to her at Rachel's party on Saturday night."

Sam looked up from the produce cart where she was straightening a display of green beans. "I didn't know you were at that party."

"Believe me, Sam, that is not my scene. Rachel's brother invited us to come. Cooper and I stopped by for a few minutes on the way to the movies, but we didn't stay long."

Sam finished with the beans and moved on to a bin of butternut squash. "It's a good thing you didn't. Things got pretty out of hand."

"That's what I heard," Annie said as she sprayed cleaner on the front of the display case. "A lot of people were already drunk when we got there. They were playing drinking games with tequila."

Sam gritted her teeth. "I hope Jamie had enough sense not to participate."

"He didn't. At least not while we were there. Sophia, now she's a different story. She was running the show, and plastered out of her mind. I'm not sure what he sees in her. She's pretty and all, but so are a lot of other girls."

"Tell that to him. Jamie respects your opinion, Annie. It would mean more coming from you."

"Believe me, I will. First chance I get to talk to him when *she's* not around."

Unfortunately that chance didn't happen when Jamie stopped in with Sophia after their lunch at the Main Street Grille.

Sophia crinkled her nose the minute she crossed the threshold. "It smells bad in here."

Jamie's expression darkened. "Obviously you haven't been in many seafood markets. Ours smells fresh compared to most others." He dragged her over to the checkout counter. "Sophia, this is my Aunt Faith and my grandmother."

Lovie came around from behind the counter. "You can call me Lovie. Everyone else does."

"Lovie?" Sophia's lip curled up in distaste. "Is that some kind of nickname?"

"Short for Louvenia." Lovie ran her hand down Sophia's auburn mane. "Aren't you the pretty one? What a shame you can't bottle this color."

Sophia brushed Lovie's hand out of the way as she lifted her hair into a ponytail.

Sam's cell phone lit up with Craig Smalls's caller ID on the counter beside the register. Reaching for the phone, she said, "Excuse me. I need to take this call from my attorney." Pressing the phone to her ear, she stepped away from the others.

"We're going to have to postpone the closing," Craig began. "There are some discrepancies with the numbers."

Her body went rigid. "I hope it doesn't have anything to do with our loan application?"

"It's nothing like that," Craig said. "Our numbers don't add up. It happens all the time. We just need to consult with Roy Cook, the loan officer at the bank. I've left a message for him to call me, but I have no way of knowing when he'll get back to me. Does it work for you and Eli to schedule the closing for two o'clock tomorrow?"

Sam's mind raced with the logistics of Eli's schedule and her staffing situation at the market. "We'll figure it out somehow. We need to close on this house, Craig. We're having our wedding reception there on Saturday."

Jamie appeared at her side. "What's wrong?" he asked, when she ended the call.

"We've postponed the closing until tomorrow at two."

"What about the sellers? Aren't they from out of town?"

"They're not coming to the closing. They've already signed and notarized the documents. Mom has a doctor's appointment at two thirty. I don't want her to cancel it, but I can't leave Faith and Annie here alone."

"I'll cover for you."

Sam nodded at Sophia. "What about her?"

"She'll survive being alone for a couple of hours." The empty cooler caught his eye. "What happened there?"

"It went out over the weekend," Sam explained. "I finally got ahold of the repairman. He should be here any minute."

"Did we lose much merchandise?"

"A fair amount," Sam said. "Roberto will have to work until midnight to make up for what we lost."

The front door swung open and a throng of customers ushered in a blast of cold air. "You need me here." Jamie took

Sophia by the elbow. "She wants to take a nap anyway. I'll run her home and come right back."

Jamie dragged Sophia out the front door before Sam could argue with him. He returned fifteen minutes later, just as the refrigerator repairman arrived. Sam had forgotten what a hard worker her son was. With his help, Roberto was able to replace the stock lost from the cooler failure and get a head start on the large number of holiday orders.

Mother and son were both exhausted when they arrived home after work. "What's all this?" she asked when she saw the moving boxes stacked along the walls in the kitchen.

Jamie beamed. "I knocked out most of the packing this morning, every room except your bedroom."

"I knew I could count on you." She kissed him on the cheek. "Let's say a prayer that we have a house to move into." She set her bag on the island and dropped to the nearest bar stool.

"Don't worry, Mom. You're gonna love the new house. Just think. We'll get to watch the sun set over the water every night."

She smiled up at him. "How is it that you can always sense how I'm feeling?"

"Because I feel the same way. For so long, it was just you and me, making our way through life together. Those years bonded us in a special way. Don't get me wrong. I'm thrilled Eli is joining our little family. But I will never forget the happy memories that belong only to us."

Tears pooled in Sam's eyes. "What a beautiful thing to say, son. And just what I needed to hear."

He kissed the top of Sam's head. "I'd better go check on our houseguest." Jamie left the kitchen and returned a minute later. "Sophia's not here."

"What do you mean, she's not here? Where could she have gone?"

"I don't know. But I just checked the whole house and she's not here."

"Maybe she went for a walk."

"It's freezing outside. Sophia is not one for roughing it."

"No surprise there." Sam slid off the bar stool and conducted her own quick survey of the house. "I don't see her purse in her room anywhere. She probably went off with one of her friends."

Jamie removed his phone from his pocket and thumbed a text. When Sophia didn't respond right away, he tried to call her. "No answer." He set the phone down on the bar. "Maybe if we're lucky she won't come back." He grinned as though he was joking, but the grim tone in his voice implied otherwise.

Sophia returned ten minutes later. "Where have you been?" Jamie asked.

"Rachel and I drove out to the beach."

That explains the pink cheeks and windblown hair, Sam thought.

Sophia crossed the kitchen, heading for her room. "Come on." She motioned for Jamie to follow her. "We need to get changed. We're meeting Rachel and some of her friends at Angelo's in fifteen minutes for pizza. There's talk of a movie afterward."

Jamie crossed the room to her like a dutiful husband.

She smiled up at him and then sniffed his shirt. "On second thought, you'd better shower first. You stink like fish."

FIFTEEN

S AM ATE A bowl of cereal for dinner before retiring to her room to start packing. She organized her clothes and folded them neatly in the boxes Jamie had left her. She didn't wait up for Jamie and Sophia, but the sound of water running in the bathroom woke her when they came in around eleven.

Jamie was waiting for her in the kitchen the following morning with a skillet of scrambled eggs. "Sophia wants to sleep late, so I figured I might as well go in early."

Sam didn't argue. She needed his help. "What's she going to do for the rest of the day?"

He shrugged. "She made plans with Rachel. They didn't talk about specifics, which is fine by me as long as she's entertained."

Sam decided not to question the weary tone in her son's voice.

When Eli came to pick her up a few minutes before two, Jamie placed an arm around each of them and walked them to the back door. "Run along now, you lovebirds. Go buy us a new house. Feel free to christen it while you're out. Just spare me the details."

Sam and Eli were rushing to the Jeep, their heads ducked against the cold, when she received a call from Craig Smalls. "I hate to be the bearer of bad news, but we're not going to be able to close today as planned."

She unlocked the car, slipped inside, and slammed the door. "What the hell is going on, Craig?"

"I can't get Roy Cook to call me back. I've left six or seven messages for him. His secretary understands the urgency of the situation and has assured me she's given him the messages. I don't know what to tell you."

She inserted her key into the ignition. "I'm already in my car. I might as well drive over to the bank and find out what's going on. I'll make sure he calls you immediately."

❋

"These things happen when you try to close a property too quickly," Roy Cook explained when Sam and Eli stormed into his office.

Eli's face flushed red. "That's not what you said when you were salivating over our loan application. We are holding our wedding luncheon in this house on Saturday. We need to take possession of it as soon as possible. What is so hard about calling our attorney back?"

Cook dropped to his desk chair with a heavy sigh. "I apologize. I don't know what to say except that I'm short-staffed. I can barely keep my head above water. I will take care of it right away."

Sam rapped her knuckles on his desk. "If my attorney doesn't hear from you within the hour, I'm pulling my business from this bank, including the Sweeney's accounts. Is that understood?"

He flinched. "Yes, ma'am."

She turned on her heels and stormed out of his office. "This is ridiculous," she said once they were back in the car. Because he's too lazy to make a phone call, we may not be able to get married."

"Oh no!" Eli's eyebrows shot up to his hairline. "We are so getting married on Saturday. As long as Pastor Paul is alive and the Creekside Chapel hasn't burned down, we are getting married."

"What are we gonna do for a reception? Serve our guests DoubleDees barbecue and baked beans in my living room surrounded by boxes?"

"Or we can have the reception another time. The ceremony is the most important thing."

Sam felt her anger melt away. "Worse case scenario, we can make the Christmas Eve party out at the farm our reception. I would hate to do it, because my family is always taking advantage of Jackie's generosity in sharing Moss Creek Farm. But we can at least consider it an option."

"See, there you go—viable backup plan number one. If that doesn't work out, we'll come up with something else." Placing his hand on the back of her neck, Eli drew her to him and kissed her hard on the lips. "As long as we have the license to prove we're married, we can make all the whoopee we want."

They realized their mistake at the same time.

Sam smacked her forehead with the palm of her hand. "We forgot about the marriage license. How could we have been so stupid?" She slumped back in her seat. "That's it then. We have no choice but to postpone the wedding."

"Not so fast." Eli pressed his phone to his ear. When

the person on the other end answered, he said, "Officer Eli Marshall calling for Chief Andrews." Andrews came on the line and Eli explained the situation. He listened for a few seconds before thanking him and hanging up. "Are you up for a road trip to Charleston? The probate judge is a friend of Chief Andrews's. He's calling him now. Chief thinks there's only a twenty-four-hour waiting period for the license, but he's gonna confirm that and let me know. We don't need a blood test, just one form of identification. A driver's license will work."

Sam put the Jeep in gear and peeled out of the bank's parking lot. "What about your shift? Aren't you supposed to be at work at four?"

"The chief is getting someone to cover for me until we get back. What about you? Can Jamie stay awhile longer at the market?"

"I'm sure he can. Sophia has plans with Rachel today. But we should text him to let him know."

Eli typed a quick text into his phone.

"All of these things are bad omens, Eli. The problems at the bank with the closing. Us forgetting to apply for a marriage license. Having SoDiva in the house is added stress when things are already so chaotic at the market. We should've waited until spring to get married. Maybe we shouldn't be getting married at all."

She sensed his body stiffen, but she kept her attention focused on the road so as to avoid seeing the disappointment on his face.

"You don't really believe that, do you?" he asked in a low worried tone.

She shook her head.

"I didn't think so." He ran his finger down her cheek. "No way I could have waited until spring to marry you. We've encountered a few bumps in the road, but come hell or high water—with or without a reception at the bungalow, even if we have to fly out to Las Vegas—we're going to exchange our vows on Saturday."

She smiled over at him. "That sounds perfect. Except the Las Vegas part, of course. I don't need a party or a house. I just need you."

SIXTEEN

THE PROCESS OF applying for a marriage license took longer than expected. The staff had already closed the market by the time Sam and Eli returned from Charleston. She let him off in the parking lot, to retrieve his cruiser for duty, and drove straight home. Jamie and Sophia were sitting at the island in the kitchen when she arrived.

Sam gave her son a quick hug. "Thanks for covering for me. I owe you one."

Frown lines crinkled along his forehead. "Please tell me you got the marriage license."

"We filled out the paperwork and paid the fee. Eli is going back Thursday morning to pick up the license." Sam opened the refrigerator and surveyed the contents. "Can I interest the two of you in some dinner?" She removed a pound of crabmeat and set it on the island. "I can throw together a crab casserole in no time."

Jamie cleared his throat. "We're—"

"We're going to eat at Rachel's." Sophia jutted out her

chin and looked Sam dead in the eye. "I hope that's not a problem for you."

The muscles in Sam's shoulders tightened. "That depends. Are her parents home from their trip yet?"

"They, um—" Jamie started.

"They got back last night," said Sophia. Seriously, Sam. Are you always this protective?"

"When it comes to my son's safety and his reputation, you bet I am. Especially after what happened Saturday night. You narrowly escaped a minor in possession charge. You may be in college, but you are still underage."

"Whatever." Sophia hopped off the bar stool and slipped on a short fur coat the color of aged brandy.

"Whoa." Jamie's jaw dropped to the counter. "Is that real?"

"Yes. It's mink." She held her arm out to him.

He stroked the sleeve. "I've never seen you wear it."

"I bought it today when Rachel and I were in Charleston. It's a Christmas gift from my parents to me." She performed a pirouette. The plush mink swung out from her torso and settled just below her hips. "I deserve it, don't you think? Since they abandoned me at Christmastime."

"Russia is the mink capital of the world," Sam said. "Won't you spoil their fun if they were planning to bring you a surprise?"

"Not at all. A girl can't have too many fur coats. They would want me to have it now anyway, since it's freezing outside." She pranced across the kitchen and opened the back door. "Let's go, Jamie. Rachel is waiting for us."

"I promise we won't be late," Jamie said to Sam as he followed Sophia out the door.

After her hectic day, Sam was relieved to have a quiet

evening to herself. She heaped a generous amount of crabmeat onto a plate, grabbed the cocktail sauce from the refrigerator and the Saltines from the pantry, and sat down at the island. She was still picking at the crab when Jamie returned home alone thirty minutes later.

Sam looked up from her plate when he came through the back door. "Where's Sophia?"

"She's spending the night at Rachel's." Still wearing his coat, Jamie popped the top off the container of crabmeat, picked out a juicy lump, and sucked it between his lips. "I didn't want to stay. It was mostly girls."

"Did you see her parents?"

"They weren't there," Jamie said, avoiding her gaze.

The skin on her neck prickled. Something at the Bennett's had made him uncomfortable. "I'm glad you decided to come home. I was feeling a little blue." She walked her plate to the sink. "Why don't I make you a proper dinner? I have some leftover chili I can heat up." She removed a bowl from the refrigerator and dumped the chili in a pot.

"Do you realize we only have three nights left in this house, Jamie? If those idiots at the bank can get our documents straightened out, that is." Sam made a mental note to check her inbox for an email from Craig. "Since this might be our last night here alone, I think we should do something special."

"Like what?" He tugged off his coat and tossed it onto a nearby moving box.

She thought about it as she stirred the chili. "I know. Why don't we play Monopoly? We could have a marathon. I might even let you win this time."

Jamie rolled his eyes. "I always beat you fair and square, and you know it."

"We haven't played in years. I deserve a chance to redeem myself."

"I don't know, Mom. Monopoly sounds kind of lame."

She filled a Dixie paper bowl with chili and slid it across the island to him. "Don't be such a Donnie Downer. It'll be fun. Beats sitting around feeling sorry for ourselves."

He plunked himself down on a nearby bar stool. "Whatever. Since there's nothing better to do."

After Jamie ate his chili, they set up the board game in front of the tree. The flames from the gas logs flickered and Christmas carols played softly in the background. Sam chatted on about the wedding and the new house, but no matter how hard she tried, she could not drive Jamie out of his funk. Whether SoDiva had rejected him or whether he sensed trouble brewing, he was not okay with leaving his girlfriend to spend the night at the Bennett's.

Jamie had obtained all the real estate on the Monopoly board and Sam was nearing bankruptcy when Eli called around ten thirty.

"Please tell me Jamie is at home with you." The grave tone in his voice alarmed her.

She smiled at Jamie. "He's sitting right here. Beating me at Monopoly as usual."

"Phew! What a relief. I've never loved that kid more than I do right now."

"What's wrong?" The sound of sirens pierced the air on Eli's end of the line. "You're scaring me, Eli. Where are you?"

"Brace yourself, Sam. I have some disturbing news. There was a bust at the Bennett's house tonight. I'm on my way to the station with Sophia. I'm charging her with possession of a controlled substance with intent to distribute."

Sam sat up straight. "Hold on a minute, Eli. What controlled substance?"

"Cocaine."

Sam threw the dice on the board and fell back against the chair cushion. "You've got to be kidding me. Cocaine? Where would she get something like that around here?"

"Apparently she and Rachel bought it from one of their sorority sisters when they went to Charleston today. Drug use is a national epidemic amongst kids this age. We've seen some in Prospect. But not much." Eli let out an audible sigh. "There's even more bad news, Sammie. An ambulance just rushed Rachel's younger brother to the hospital with an apparent overdose."

SEVENTEEN

"I KNEW SOMETHING WAS wrong at Rachel's," Jamie admitted on the way to the police station. "Sophia made it obvious she didn't want me there. Now I know why. She knows how much I hate drugs." He raked his hands through his dark hair. "A little weed is one thing, but cocaine? That blows my mind. I know kids at school who have tried it. I never guessed Sophia would be one of them."

Sam paid close attention to the road as she navigated the back streets to the police station. "I need to know, Jamie. How much do you care about this girl?"

"I don't care about her at all, Mom. I don't even like her."

"Then why did you invite her for Christmas?"

"Honestly, she invited herself." Jamie stared out the window at the colorful lights that adorned the houses in their neighborhood. "I felt sorry for her when she told me her parents weren't taking her with them to Russia. She seemed so sad. She didn't have anywhere else to go. What kind of parents go off and leave their only child alone for the holidays?"

Sam shook her head. "Not very nice ones."

"Sophia is so pretty and popular. She can have anybody she wants. I was flattered when she picked me. Although looking back, I think she was interested in me because of my position on the baseball team. I feel really stupid for letting her use me like that."

"That's what she is, son. A user. And you were her latest victim. This is one of many upsets you'll experience on your journey through life." She reached for his hand. "Learn from it, but don't let it drag you down."

They parked the car in front of the station and went inside. Sam checked in with the desk sergeant. "Will you let Eli know we're here, please."

"He might be awhile, Sam. His hands are pretty full. They brought in a paddy wagon full of your friends." Sergeant Miller directed his gaze at Jamie. "Good thing you had the sense to go home early."

"They're not my friends," Jamie mumbled, staring down at his feet.

"Just tell Eli we're here," Sam said, and turned her back on the desk sergeant.

Fifteen minutes later, Eli sought them out in the waiting room. Sam and Jamie stood to face him.

"Sophia is in a lot of trouble," Eli said. "I'm sorry, but I can't let you take her home tonight."

"We don't want to take her home," Sam said. "Not tonight. Not ever. That girl crossed a line. I should feel responsible for her because she's staying under my roof, but I don't. Not anymore. Her parents flew halfway around the world for the holidays. They left their daughter, knowing she was coming here, but they didn't even bother to call me to introduce themselves, or explain their situation. Or to say thank you. They could've at least sent a fruit cake."

Eli turned his attention to Jamie. "Do you feel the same way about Sophia?"

"Hell yes, I feel the same way. I had no idea she was such a screwed-up bitch when I invited her here. She's done nothing but cause trouble since we got home. And I'm not just talking about the cocaine. I don't care if you lock her up forever. Throw away the key while you're at it."

"What a mess," Eli said, rubbing his temples. "Sophia asked me to call you. She's under the impression the two of you will bail her out."

"Tell her to call her parents," Sam said.

"She claims she doesn't know where they're staying in Moscow. She says their cell phones aren't working."

"That's a lie," Jamie said. "I know for a fact that she talked to her mother yesterday."

"Why don't I let the two of you talk to her?" Eli suggested. "Maybe *you* can convince her that calling her parents is her best option."

"Okay," Jamie agreed. "What about Rachel? Is she being charged?"

"Yes. She's up to her neck with Sophia."

"Is her brother going to die?" Jamie asked.

"Honestly, Jamie, I don't know. A lot depends on how much cocaine he used."

Eli led them to an interrogation room at the back of the station. Sophia was sitting alone at a rectangular table with wild eyes, disheveled hair, and mascara smeared down her cheeks.

The classic mug shot photo.

Sam and Jamie took seats in the chairs opposite her.

"Good move, Soph," he said. "If I'd known you were a coke whore, we would have had a very different conversation when you invited yourself to come home with me for Christmas."

"Shut up, Jamie!" she snapped. "Are you going to bail me out or not?"

"Not," Jamie said so matter of factly Sam wanted to hug him.

Sophia turned her attention to Sam. "Will you loan me the money until my parents get home from their trip?"

Sam shook her head. "I'm sorry. From what Eli says, your case is more complicated than that."

Placing his hands on the table, Eli leaned in close to Sophia. "You seem to be having a difficult time grasping the enormity of your situation. Which is why I asked Sam and Jamie here to help you understand. You will have to appear in front of the magistrate tomorrow morning. He will decide whether to set bail. You had more than two grams of cocaine in your purse. Possession of a controlled substance with intent to sell is a felony in the state of South Carolina. For first-time offenders with no prior charges, a conviction carries up to a twenty-five-thousand-dollar fine and a possible fifteen-year prison sentence."

"I already told you." Sophia pounded the table with her fist. "I wasn't selling cocaine to anyone. I was giving it away."

Jamie stared at her with a slack jaw. "Are you really that stupid? Or are you just high?"

Eli shot Jamie a look that shut him up. He turned back to Sophia. "Sell or distribute, we use the words interchangeably.

If Rachel's brother doesn't recover, you may be looking at manslaughter charges as well."

"It's not my fault he snorted so much," Sophia snapped. "I tried to tell the kid to slow down."

Sam forced herself to sound calm. "Regardless of what you think about this situation, Sophia, you are in a lot of trouble and you really do need your parents' help. Do you have an aunt or friend of the family who might know how to get in touch with them?"

Sophia shook her head.

Jamie fell back in his chair. "Give it up, Soph. I heard you talking to your mother on the phone yesterday."

The tears trickled out at first, and then Sophia lost it and began to sob. Dropping down to the nearest chair, Eli slid a box of tissues across the table to her. Sam watched the clock while Jamie twiddled his thumbs. After five minutes, the sobbing subsided.

"Are you ready to call your parents?" Sam asked.

Sophia peered up at Sam through wet eyelashes. "Will you do it?"

"I don't think . . .," Sam started, but then realized how much she'd relish the opportunity to give the girl's parents an earful. The Raineys had been gallivanting around Russia while she'd been dealing with their spoiled brat. "Fine." Sam reached in her bag for her phone. "Do you know the name of their hotel in Moscow?"

Sophia jotted down a number on the pad of paper in front of her and shot it across the table to Sam. "This is my dad's cell number. He's at home. In California."

Sam did a double take. "What did you just say?"

Sophia's chin quivered. "My parents never went to Russia."

Sam suddenly found it difficult to breathe. "You mean to tell me you've been lying to us this whole time?"

"It was not that hard, Sam. You're pretty gullible." Sophia blew her nose. "But you might as well know the truth now because Daddy's going to tell you anyway. I got in an argument with my parents during Thanksgiving. They took away my car and grounded me for Christmas break."

"Let me guess," Eli said. "Your parents caught you using drugs."

Sophia hung her head.

Sam fought down a wave of nausea. "So you asked my son if you could come here instead, where you wouldn't be grounded. You deserve everything that's coming to you, young lady." She read the number off the pad of paper and punched it into her phone.

Sophia's father answered on the third ring. "Oliver Rainey." Sam could barely hear him above the voices in the background on his end of the line.

"Mr. Rainey, this is Samantha Sweeney, Jamie's mother, calling from South Carolina. Your daughter has been staying with us for the past few days. I'm afraid I have some bad news. She's been arrested. I'm with her at the police department now."

"I'm sorry to hear that." Mr. Rainey lowered his voice and Sam had to listen closer to hear him over his guests. "There's not much I can do from here this time of night. Bail her out, and I'll have my attorney contact you in the morning."

His eloquent and calculating speech summoned, in Sam's mind, the image of a distinguished man in his midfifties with gray hair and ice blue eyes like his daughter's.

"I can't do that, Mr. Rainey. Even if I wanted to, which

I definitely do not. Sophia is scheduled to appear before the magistrate in the morning. He will decide whether or not to grant her bail. The police are charging your daughter with possession of cocaine with intent to distribute."

Sophia's father made no response. But the clinking of ice cubes and laughter in the background assured Sam that he was still on the line. Finally, he whispered, "Did you say cocaine?"

"Yes, sir. Cocaine."

"Hold on a minute. Let me get to my study." The line grew quiet as he moved away from the party. Footsteps echoed on a marble floor. A door closed, a lock clicked, and he came back on the line. "Ms. Sweeney, I've never known my daughter to do drugs until she started dating your son. I blame him for this. I'm sorry, but I've forgotten his name."

Sam gripped the phone tighter. "You mean to tell me you allowed your daughter to spend Christmas with a boy, and you don't even know his name?"

"My daughter has a lot of friends, Ms. Sweeney. I have a hard time keeping up with all of them."

"For your information, Mr. Rainey, my son, *Jamie*, was at home playing Monopoly with me tonight. Sophia was at Rachel Bennett's house at the time of the arrest. Rachel is one of her sorority sisters."

"I know who Rachel Bennett is," he snapped. "She came out to California to visit us last summer."

"Well then, you may remember that Rachel has a younger brother. Charlie Bennett was rushed to the hospital earlier with an apparent drug overdose. We haven't received an update on his condition. If he doesn't survive, god forbid, Sophia and Rachel could be facing manslaughter charges."

"That's unfortunate. I wish him the best," he said without

a trace of concern in his voice. "Regardless of whether your son was arrested or not, I hold him responsible for getting my daughter into trouble."

"I can assure you, Mr. Rainey, Sophia didn't need anyone's help. She got into this trouble all on her own. Are you aware that in the state of South Carolina, if convicted, the charge for possession of cocaine with intent to distribute carries a fifteen-year sentence? Never mind the twenty–five-thousand-dollar fine. Your daughter could go to prison for a very long time."

"I'll call my attorney now and have him contact one of his associates on the East Coast first thing in the morning. I'm hosting a dinner party, Ms. Sweeney. I need to get back to my guests. That's the best I can do tonight."

A sharp pain struck Sam's temple. "Your best explains a lot of things, Mr. Rainey. I'd never met your daughter until this past Friday." She set her eyes on Sophia. "But I find her spoiled, self-centered, and rude. I'm pretty sure she didn't get that way on her own."

Another brief period of silence ensued. "If I leave now, I can make the red-eye."

"I'm sure Sophia will be relieved to see you." Sam straightened. "Charleston is the nearest airport to Prospect. Google it. I'll text you my address. Jamie and I will pack up Sophia's things and leave them on the front porch for you to pick up tomorrow."

EIGHTEEN

Eli TOOTED HIS car horn for Sam at ten minutes before nine on Wednesday morning. She rushed to the curb, her head ducked against the gusts of wind. "Good grief, it's cold outside," she said, sliding into the passenger side of his cruiser.

He leaned across the console and pecked her on the cheek. "According to the weatherman, this arctic front has settled in until after the new year."

"Great. Knowing our luck, it'll snow this weekend and bring our wedding plans to a screeching halt."

He snorted. "I don't think that's anything you need to worry about. We live in the Lowcountry. The only white on the ground you're gonna see is the sand on the beaches."

"I wouldn't be so sure about that," Sam said, her jaw set. "It's happened before. In my early twenties, we had an epic snowstorm during the days leading up to Christmas. The whole town was rendered immobile for a week."

Eli ran his hand across the stubble on his chin. "I'd

forgotten about that. My parents took us to Colorado skiing that Christmas. We were envious when we found out our friends were blanketed under eight inches of snow." He kissed the tip of her nose. "I told you, nothing is going to prevent us from getting married on Saturday." He put the car in gear and pulled away from the curb. "Let's go close this thing. Have you heard whether the documents are ready?"

"I received an email last night when I got home from the police station. According to Craig, the documents are ready, and everything is set to go." She rubbed her hands together in front of the heat vent. "Have you been by the station this morning? I'm curious how SoDiva survived her night in lockup."

"No, but I talked to dispatch a few minutes ago. She nearly drove the guards crazy, making unreasonable requests for feather pillows and cheeseburgers with fries. Her father is scheduled to arrive around noon with a hotshot attorney from Atlanta. They postponed her hearing with the magistrate until he gets here." Eli looked both ways before making a right-hand turn on Main. "I noticed the suitcase on your front porch. Sophia's, I presume. I didn't think you were serious when you were talking to her father."

Sam smiled. "Believe it or not, that wasn't me. Jamie is the one who packed her bags last night when we got home. He can hardly wait to get her out of his life."

❋

Their meeting at the bank took less than an hour. Back in the car, Eli dropped the four sets of house keys in the cup holder. "I don't know about you, but I'm relieved to have that over with." He fastened his seat belt and turned on the ignition. "Do you have time to run by the house on your way to work?"

She glanced at the clock. Five minutes until the market opened. "I wish I could. But I should get to work. I'm sure we'll be slammed from the get-go today."

"I understand." He backed out of the parking place and pulled onto Main Street. "I figured I'd moved my stuff in the next few days so I can help you with yours after the wedding."

"I thought you were going to Charleston to pick up the marriage license this morning."

"That won't take but a couple of hours. I'll be back by one at the latest, which will give me time to drop these shower gifts off and move some of my clothes."

Sam pressed her fingers to her lips to hide her smile. "I'm sorry, Eli. I totally forgot about the gifts."

"Don't worry. You get to write the thank you notes." He winked at her. "I have the night shift again tonight, but I'm hoping Jamie will help me move my furniture after work tomorrow."

"What furniture? You're only allowed to bring your bed into this marriage. The rest of your stuff is junk." Eli had inherited a queen-size rice bed from his parents that had been in his family for generations. Everything else was slated for Goodwill.

A naughty twinkle glistened in his eye. "I can't wait to see your sexy, naked body lying in my bed on Saturday night. In our new house. With the moon shining through the windows. You and me, husband and wife."

Sam's body grew rigid. "What about Jamie? I can't just ditch him on Christmas Eve. I thought we agreed to wait until after the wedding to move in."

Eli frowned. "I don't remember agreeing to anything. I'm not even sure we ever talked about our wedding night."

They rode in silence until they reached the stoplight at Main and Creekside.

"I'm sorry, Eli. Jamie is an adult. He knows what goes on behind bedroom doors. It's gonna be awkward for me. And for him."

"And for me. It'll be awkward for all three of us the first night, regardless of where we sleep. Even more so for me if we stay at your house. I've slept on your couch many a night, but I'd feel like an intruder if I slept in your bed, in your room, with you. My apartment is too small, so that's out of the question. At least at the new house everything will be different for all three of us. The preconceptions work in our favor. Jamie is expecting us to share the master bedroom."

"You make a good point. But Heidi is banking on the house being empty for the wedding brunch. We can't have our guests tripping over moving boxes. Why the sudden rush to move in?"

"I'm excited. That's all. And, if we move a little each day, it'll be easier in the long run." He turned left into the parking lot at the market and pulled into an empty space. He shifted toward her, taking her face in his hands and kissing her lips. "Let's not argue. Everything will fall into place. We've been through a lot this week. We'll be so tired it won't matter where we sleep on Christmas Eve as long as we have a place to rest our heads."

"And a Christmas tree for our gifts," she said, kissing him back. "Even if we have to sit on the floor while we open them."

"That's my girl." He held his hand up for a high five.

"Now get in there and get to work. Leave the wedding night plans to me."

✳

Two unexpected guests paid Sam a visit at the market on Wednesday afternoon. Despite the dark shadows under his eyes, Oliver Rainey was every bit as elegant as she'd imagined. Judging from his attire—red cashmere sweater, gray flannel slacks, and Gucci loafers—he'd driven straight from his dinner party to the airport, while Sophia looked as though she'd traveled to hell and back. She peeked through her curtain of dank hair, like rust-colored draperies in an outdated hotel room, and Sam could see her face was splotchy from crying.

"I hope you don't mind us barging in on you like this," Rainey said, observing the crowded showroom. "I can see you're busy. We won't take but a minute of your time."

Jamie came out from the back and introduced himself to Oliver Rainey with a firm handshake. He turned to Sophia. "I see they let you out on bail. I hope that means you're going home. Your suitcase is on my front porch."

"We already picked it up," Rainey said. "Thank you. We're on our way to the airport now. But Sophia has something she'd like to say to both of you before we leave."

Sophia hung her head and stared down at her feet. "Sorry," she mumbled.

Jamie flinched. "Nothing against you, Mr. Rainey. We've only just met. But after what your daughter put us through, her apology means nothing to me."

An expression Sam interpreted as approval crossed Rainey's handsome face. "I understand, young man. You have every right to feel that way." He tapped his daughter on the shoulder. "Go wait for me in the car."

Shoulders slumped and head bowed, she exited through the front door.

"Is there somewhere we can speak in private?" Rainey asked.

Sam cast a quick glance at the checkout counter, stopping short when she came upon her mother's prying eyes peering at them over the cash register. "Let's go in the back." Sam led Rainey and Jamie through the kitchen to the office. She did not offer him a seat. "I have only a minute."

"I understand." Rainey inhaled a deep breath. "I'm hoping you can shed some light on my daughter's situation. You"— he nodded at Jamie—"more than your mother. Needless to say, I'm concerned about the charges. I haven't seen any evidence of drug abuse. I'm aware of her recreational use. She came home so high on something over Thanksgiving we took away her car and grounded her. But I haven't seen any signs of addiction. Her grades aren't suffering and her spending habits haven't changed."

"If you're asking me if I think Sophia should go to rehab, the answer is no," Jamie said. "I think she's bored and looking for a thrill."

"Or attention," Sam added.

"Or both," Oliver Rainey said in a resigned tone. "In the grand scheme of things, that's the best answer I could hope for." He held his hand out to them in turn. "I apologize for any inconvenience my daughter has caused you. If there's any way I can make amends."

When he reached for his wallet, Sam held her hand up. "Thanks, but no. Take your daughter home. Get her some help. She may not need rehab for drug addiction, but she sure as hell needs to rehab her attitude."

"I admire your spunk, Ms. Sweeney. Not many people would have the courage to speak their minds to me the way you did last night and today. Believe me when I tell you, I heard every word."

❋

Lovie cornered Sam behind the fish counter the first opportunity she found. "What's going on? Was that Sophia's father? Did something happen to make her leave? Jamie didn't do anything to hurt her, did he?"

"Geez, Mom. You know your grandson better than that. Sophia got herself into trouble. We were forced to call her parents. Jamie and Sophia are no longer dating. And that's all I'm going to say on the matter." Sam spun on her heels and went back to work.

Customers were lined up three deep at the counter when Sam's second visitor marched in around four. "I need a word with you, Samantha Sweeney." Donna Bennett stood before her with her arms crossed.

"I'm sorry, but you'll have to wait your turn." Sam took her time in finishing up with her customers.

"Give her hell, Sammie," Faith whispered as Sam walked from behind the counter to greet Donna.

"Let's talk outside." Taking her by the arm, Sam dragged Donna out the front door.

On the sidewalk out front, Donna said, "But it's cold out here," and wrapped her cashmere cape tighter around her ample body.

"Good! We'll keep the conversation short. In fact, let's

talk while I walk you to your car." Sam took off toward the parking lot.

Trailing behind her, Donna called out a string of expletives, but the wind carried them off before they reached Sam's ears. Sam turned to face her when they arrived at Donna's Mercedes sedan. "Go ahead, Donna. Speak your piece."

Donna towered over Sam, pinning her against the car. "I'm holding *your* son responsible for everything that happened at my house last night. Did you know that *my* son nearly died? My *son*," she repeated, particles of spit spewing from her lips.

Sam pushed the woman off her. "For the record, I'm glad Charlie is okay," she said, wiping the spit from her face with the corner of her apron. "But I don't see how you can blame Jamie for what happened at *your* house last night. He wasn't even there. He was at home—"

"I know. I heard. He was at home with you playing Monopoly. Mamby pamby mama's boy that he is." Donna jabbed a finger at Sam's nose. "But that doesn't make him any less responsible. It's not fair that he gets off scot-free when my daughter might have to go to jail. Bottom line, he's responsible for bringing that piece of garbage to our quiet little town. If not for Sophia . . . "

Sam stiffened her spine, lifting herself to her full height. "You are way out of line, Donna Bennett. Sophia is Rachel's sorority sister. They were friends long before Jamie arrived on the scene. Your daughter drove Sophia to Charleston yesterday where, according to my sources, they purchased drugs from yet another one of their sorority sisters who lives there. Jamie had no part in any of that. He was working here all day. If you want someone to blame, look in the mirror. You were asking for trouble by leaving your underage children at home alone during Christmas break. I understand the police called you after they busted the party at your house on Saturday night. If you had come home then, this whole ugly mess could have been avoided."

"Why should I have to cut my trip short? I had front row seats to see the Rockettes."

Sam's eyebrows shot up. "So that's where you were, in New York?"

"My husband and I go every year during the week before Christmas, as if it's any of your business," Donna said, the sagging skin on her chin waggling as she bobbed her head.

Sam palmed her forehead. "Excuse the hell out of me for wondering why you wouldn't take your children with you to see the Rockettes at Radio City Music Hall." Sam didn't wait for Donna's response. She turned her back on her and marched back inside.

NINETEEN

H EIDI CALLED SAM early Thursday morning and requested a meeting to finalize the details of the wedding luncheon. "Would four o'clock this afternoon work for you?"

"That should be fine." Sam wasn't keen on leaving the market short-staffed, but she wanted to make certain everything was in order for the reception. "Why don't we meet at the Island Bakery across the street?"

"Perfect. And bring Annie along if you can. She's an important factor in making your reception a success."

"Don't you think you're giving her too much credit? I agree, she's talented, but she's only sixteen years old."

"Not at all. I am truly in awe of her creativity. I've found her ideas fresh and unique. And that's high praise coming from me. I've been planning parties for a long time."

"In that case, I'll make sure she comes with me."

The market was slammed all day, but business had slacked off some when Sam and Annie left a few minutes before four.

"We won't be gone long. Thirty minutes tops," she said to Lovie and Faith. "Call Jamie out from the back if you need him. And we're right across the street if you get swamped." She wrapped her wool scarf around her neck and pulled her knit hat down over her head. She opened the door to a gush of frozen air. "Come on, let's hurry." She took Annie by the hand and they dashed across the street to the bakery.

Jackie and Heidi were waiting for them in a corner booth near the window with four frothy mugs of hot cocoa on the table in front of them. Annie slid in next to Heidi and Sam joined her sister on the opposite side.

"Jackie and I were just talking about the weather," Heidi said. "I had hoped to build fires in the pits on the terrace during the luncheon, but I doubt anyone will want to be outside as cold as it is."

"Especially not on Saturday," Annie said.

Sam frowned. "Why? Is it supposed to rain? I haven't seen the forecast."

"Not rain. Snow! Yippee." Annie clapped her hands and bounced up and down like a three-year old on her way to the zoo.

"That's just great." Sam collapsed against the bench. "My wedding is ruined. We don't have snowplows in the Lowcountry. No one will be able to come."

Jackie gave Annie a warning look. "Don't worry, honey." She reached for Sam's hand and squeezed it. "They're only calling for snow showers. And yes, we do have snowplows in the Lowcountry."

"Besides, everyone we know owns a four-wheel drive," Annie added.

"True. And there's nothing I can do about the weather

anyway." Sam shook off her concern. "A little snow might even make the day more festive." She removed a set of keys from her bag. "I stopped by the bungalow after work last night. It took me ten minutes to figure out which key unlocks the front door. This is the one that works. I marked it with electrical tape." She showed Heidi the marked key before dropping it into the palm of her outstretched hand.

Heidi placed the keys in her bag and opened the folder on the table in front of her. "Our plans for the reception are coming together nicely. I hope you'll be pleased."

Sam clasped her hands together. "I can hardly wait."

"Do you still want us to surprise you?" Annie asked. "I would feel better if you approved the menu. I know how particular you are about food."

Jackie winked at Annie. "I believe 'fussy' is the word you used earlier."

Annie's hue deepened to a shade of red the color of Santa's suit.

Sam leered at her sister over the brim of her cocoa mug. "Leave Annie alone. It pays to be fussy in our line of work, doesn't it, Annie?"

Annie shook her head up and down, her honey-colored pony tail rebounding off her shoulders.

"I'm with Annie on this," Heidi said. "I would feel better if you looked at the menu. If there's anything you don't like, we still have time to make changes." She held out a sheet of rectangular card stock to Sam. "We had a menu printed for each place setting."

Sam started to reach for the menu, and then immediately snatched her hand back. "Nope. I don't need to see it. I trust Annie. She understands my likes and dislikes when it comes to food. I'm marrying my man on Saturday morning. As long as I have my family with me to celebrate, you can feed me rotten eel and I won't know the difference."

"Okay then. Rotten eel it is." Heidi smiled and placed the menu back in her folder. She consulted the notepad in her file. "Flowers are next on the list. I've ordered a few stems from a local florist, a delightful older gentleman by the name of Felipe Marsh at Waterside Flowers. He told me you ordered the poinsettias for the church from him. I talked him into giving you the wholesale price, by the way." Heidi paused, clearing her throat. "We know how busy you are at work. Would you like for us to take the poinsettias to the church for you?"

"We can arrange them on the altar, and make them look pretty," Jackie added.

Sam shifted her gaze back and forth between Jackie and Heidi. "The two of you are up to something. I can tell by the stupid grins on your faces. Do whatever you'd like to the altar. All I ask is that you keep it simple."

"Simple is my middle name," Jackie said.

Sam nearly choked on her cocoa. "You're about as simple as I am sophisticated." She set her mug down and wiped her mouth. "Seriously, though, I appreciate all your efforts. All three of you." She looked at each of them in turn. "You have carte blanche to do whatever you'd like as long as you stick as close as possible to the budget."

"Hmm." Jackie pursed her lips. "Carte blanche on a budget? That's a new one for me."

Annie slid closer to Heidi, peering over her shoulder at the file. "You know, I've been thinking. Maybe we should take this off the menu and add . . ." She whispered something in Heidi's ear.

Jackie leaned into Sam. "I'm just teasing you about the budget. Everything is going to be beautiful. I promise. I've recommended Heidi to several of my clients, and they've all been pleased with every aspect of her event planning."

Sam considered the unlikely friends across the table, one young and one old, their heads close together, lost in their own private conversation. "Annie certainly seems to approve of her. She talks about her nonstop."

"Annie will learn a lot from Heidi."

Sam smiled. "And vice versa."

Jackie nudged Sam with her elbow. "I hear things didn't work out so well with Sophia. I hope Jamie isn't heartbroken."

"News travels fast in this town."

"News can travel from here to China in seconds, Sammie. Or haven't you noticed?"

"Actually, I haven't. I do my best to avoid all avenues of social media." Sam narrowed her eyes as she looked through the window at the market across the street, checking to make certain a line hadn't formed out the front door. "I think mostly Jamie is relieved. I'm not sure he ever truly cared about Sophia. She is popular and beautiful, and he was flattered when she set her sights on him. He learned a lot from the experience. We both did."

"Like I tell my boys—the lessons we learn the hardest are the ones that teach us the most."

TWENTY

LITTLE PRODUCT REMAINED on the shelves at Sweeney's by closing time on Friday. The line of customers waiting to pick up their special orders for their holiday feasts had stretched around the building for most of the day. The loyal patrons did not complain about having to wait in the cold. They were grateful for the services Sweeney's provided, even more so when Sam was able to satisfy their last-minute requests—a pint of oysters or pound of crabmeat they'd suddenly realized they needed. Her projections had been spot-on. The Christmas season at Captain Sweeney's was deemed a success. The staff left with healthy bonuses in their pockets and a weekend off to enjoy the holiday with their families before returning bright and early Monday morning to do it all over again for New Year's.

Sam drove straight home, luxuriated in a hot shower until her fingers and toes wrinkled, and dressed in her warmest flannel pajamas. She heated up a container of chicken noodle soup and brewed a cup of Twinings Pure Peppermint tea. No sooner had she settled into a holiday movie on Lifetime than her doorbell rang. She slurped down another spoonful of soup before going to answer the door.

"What are you doing here?" she said, when she saw Faith shivering on her front porch.

"I have a gift for you." Faith thrust a shirt-size box wrapped in white paper with a silver ribbon at her. "It's personal. I didn't want to give it to you at work with everyone else around."

Sam took the gift from her with one hand and pulled her sister through the door with the other. "Get in here. It's freezing out there. Your lips are turning blue."

Sam took the present back to the sofa. "Can I get you something, some tea maybe?"

"No, I'm fine. I didn't mean to interrupt your dinner," Faith said, when she saw the soup bowl on the coffee table. "I can't stay long anyway. Mike is cooking steaks on the grill."

"In this weather? I call that dedication."

Faith removed her coat and planted herself in the chair next to the sofa. "You should see him! All dressed up like an Eskimo in his parka with gloves on his hands and muffs on his ears and a cherry-red scarf around his neck that matches his face."

Sam laughed out loud. "I can totally picture it. He's such a dear man." She settled back against the cushions with the gift on her lap. "Tell me, Faith. Are you happy?"

Faith hugged herself, a dreamy expression appearing on her face. "I never thought it possible to be this happy. And you will be happy too with Eli." She tilted her head to the side. "You're not having doubts, are you?"

Sam straightened. "Not a one. I've never been so sure

about anything in my life." She ripped the wrapping paper off the present and lifted the lid. "Ooh . . . This is pretty." She removed a sheer lacy negligee and matching robe.

"Every bride needs something special for her wedding night. And I know you. This is the last thing you would ever buy for yourself."

"You're right about that." Sam sprang to her feet and waltzed around the room with the negligee gripped to her torso. "I've never owned anything so feminine. I love the way it flows."

"You're gonna make a beautiful bride, Sammie. You deserve all the happiness in the world."

"Thank you so much for the sexy gift." She leaned down and kissed her sister's cheek. "You made my night. And you will make Eli's night too—tomorrow night." She folded the negligee and placed it back in the box. "I've been sitting here feeling sorry for myself because I'm alone on the night before my wedding. Eli and Jamie are off somewhere, doing lord knows what, and Jackie is at the bungalow with Heidi and Annie getting ready for the reception."

"You are exactly where you need to be tonight, resting up for your big day tomorrow." Faith eyed her soup. "Now eat your dinner before it gets cold."

Sam picked up the bowl and lifted the spoon.

"Speaking of the bungalow, I've just come from there. Jackie has the whole family working, including Mama and the twins. She made me swear I wouldn't give anything away, but I think it's safe to say it's gorgeous—a winter wonderland reception."

A wide smile spread across Sam's face. "I just got that

funny feeling in my tummy. What did we use to call them when we were little?"

"Tummy tingles. Just wait until tomorrow. Those tingles will become tremors." Faith rested her hands in her lap and twiddled her thumbs. "I'm concerned about Annie, that her current infatuation is getting out of hand."

Sam gazed at her sister over her soup spoon. "You mean with Cooper?"

"Not Cooper. Don't get me wrong. She's totally smitten with him. Their relationship is sweet, both of them so innocent. But that's normal. He's her boyfriend. I'm talking about Heidi. Annie has gone gaga over that woman."

Sam drank the remaining broth from the bowl, and then set it down on the coffee table.

"I wouldn't do that in front of Eli if I were you. You might scare him off."

She licked her lips. "Eli has seen a hell of a lot worse than my bad table manners. And he's marrying me anyway." Sam tucked her feet beneath her and stared up at the ceiling. "I know what you mean though about Heidi and Annie. They disappear to a world of their own when they're together. But they have a lot in common. As an event planner, Heidi represents all the things Annie loves—like cooking and flowers and entertaining."

"I understand that part of it." Faith leaned forward in her chair. "Look, I've only met Heidi a couple of times. She seems nice enough. My concern is more from Annie's perspective. She's still vulnerable from losing her father. I watched her tonight, the way she interacts with Heidi. Her behavior borders on hero worship. We welcomed Annie into our family after Allen died, because we love her and she's a special girl with a lot to offer. I don't want Annie to be so trusting, to expect that kind of relationship with everyone she meets."

"You're overthinking the situation, Faith. I understand your concern. Heidi is new to town and we don't know much about her past. But I get the impression she has Annie's best interests at heart."

"I hope you're right." Faith stood to go. "Maybe I just need to get to know her better."

"I think you'll like her when you do." Sam followed her sister to the door. "We can't protect our children from all life's bumps and bruises. We need to let them venture out on their own. They're gonna get stung. This situation with Sophia is a perfect example. Jamie learned a valuable lesson about life. Sure, he got his feelings hurt, but he won't be so quick to fall for the next girl based on her looks and popularity."

"Poor Jamie. I can't imagine how anyone could treat him that way." Faith slipped on her coat and reached for the door-knob. "Thanks for the pep talk. I'm not sure I'm cut out for parenting a teenager."

"You're doing great, Faith. No parent knows what they're doing when it comes to raising teenagers. It's all trial and error."

❄

Faith was pulling away from the curb when Eli and Jamie drove up in a small U-Haul moving truck. Sam held the door open for them as they dashed in out of the cold. "I was wondering what the two of you were up to? You're not seriously moving furniture tonight, are you?"

"Yep." Jamie handed her a slip of notepaper. "Aunt Jackie sent us over on a mission. She says these are your best pieces of furniture, that they will help the house look cozy without taking up too much space. She wants us to move them to the bungalow tonight."

Sam deciphered her sister's scrawl. The list included her antique settee, mahogany dresser, and walnut huntboard. "Good grief. This is half of what I own."

Jamie snatched the list back and hustled about the house gathering the items he could lift alone and setting them beside the front door.

Taking her by the elbow, Eli bent down and kissed Sam on the lips. "Your sister is barking orders right and left. None of us is brave enough to question her motives. Jamie and I just finished moving my bed. She gave me explicit instructions on how to make it up in the morning."

Sam placed her hands on her hips. "I can't believe you're not going to wait for me to spend the first night in our new home."

He leaned in closer to her. "I wanted to make sure the bed was in place for our wedding night." He planted a series of kisses on her neck.

She pushed him away. "We talked about this, Eli. I'm not leaving my son alone here on Christmas Eve."

"Jamie," Eli called out. "Did you forget to tell your mom about the plans for tomorrow night?"

Jamie returned from Sam's room with her bedside table. "I guess maybe I did." He set the table down with the other furniture. "Aunt Jackie invited me to spend the night at the farm after the Christmas Eve party."

She furrowed her brow as she considered the idea. "But we've always been together on Christmas Eve."

"I'll come over first thing on Christmas morning." He

quickly added, "Maybe not first thing, but definitely before noon. We can open our gifts and then cook a big brunch. Which reminds me, we need the gifts." He disappeared into the kitchen and returned with a handful of black garbage bags. He dropped to his knees and began filling the bag with gifts.

Sam imagined her wedding night, wrapped in Eli's arms wearing her new negligee. "Are you sure?" she asked her son.

"Yes!" He tied off the bag and popped open another one. "Apparently, they have quite the party out at the farm after Aunt Jackie goes to bed. Uncle Bill and the twins stay up late waiting for"—Jamie stopped stuffing gifts in the bag long enough to use air quotes—"Santa Claus. Last year Uncle Bill let the twins have some of his fifty-year-old single malt scotch."

Sam snickered. "In that case, how can I say no? I wouldn't want you to miss out on the opportunity to male bond with Santa Claus."

Jamie flung a trash bag over each shoulder. "I'll run these out to the truck. Then we can get the big stuff."

Sam leaned against the door and surveyed the room. "I was already depressed being alone here on the night before my wedding. Now you're taking away my furniture *and* my Christmas gifts."

"I guess that means you'll have to go to bed early." Eli ran his finger down her cheek. "I want you all rested up for tomorrow night."

TWENTY-ONE

HEAVY GRAY CLOUDS filled the sky on Saturday morning. Sam peeked through the window blinds beside her bed, and then snuggled deeper beneath her down comforter, relishing the warmth. She was as mentally prepared as she would ever be to start on this new path in her journey of life, but she wanted to savor the final moments alone. Her bed, her room, her house.

She'd been single her entire life. She was set in her ways. What if she discovered she wasn't cut out for marriage? What if she couldn't adapt to living with another person? She dismissed the feelings of doubt and allowed her mind to wander back to Jamie's childhood—the late nights when he'd crawled into her bed terrified from a nightmare or a thunderstorm, and the early mornings when he'd woken her with his little boy bad breath.

She was dozing off several minutes later when Jamie burst into the room. "Mom! It's snowing."

"Funny, ha ha. April fool's and all that." Sam rolled onto her side with her back facing the window.

"I'm serious, Mom. Look." He yanked open the blinds. "The flakes are tiny, but it's not sleet or ice. It's snow."

Sam rolled onto her back and cracked an eyelid. A fine veil of precipitation was falling outside, coating the grass, tree branches, sidewalks, and roads in white. A vision flashed before her. She was standing at the altar alone, surrounded by dozens of white poinsettias. No other family members or friends were in attendance.

She should have gone with the red poinsettia.

She sat up in bed. "That's it then. We'll have to postpone the wedding."

Jamie's jaw hit the floor. "Why would we do that?"

"Because no one will be able to make it to the chapel."

"Seriously, Mom. Six of the nine cars in this family have four-wheel drive."

"We're Southerners, Jamie. Just because we have four-wheel drive doesn't mean we know how to handle a car in the snow." Kicking back the covers, Sam unplugged her phone from the charger on the floor beside her bed, and staggered to the kitchen. She set a mug in her Keurig, and scanned the forecast on her weather app while she waited for her coffee to brew. "They're calling for four to six inches," she said to Jamie when he entered the kitchen. "That will paralyze this town. We might as well call the whole thing off now, and save everyone the trouble."

Placing his hands on her shoulders, Jamie directed Sam to the nearest bar stool. "Take some deep breaths and count to ten. Everything's gonna be fine." When her coffee finished brewing, he added a few drops of cream and a packet of sweetener, and slid it across the island to her.

"Let's turn on the local weather." Sam pointed at the empty shelf where the television usually sat. "What happened to the TV?" She glanced around the room, realizing for the first time that all the boxes and small appliances were gone. She hopped off the bar stool and circled the house. Their beds were the only furniture remaining in the house. The Christmas tree stood abandoned in the corner of the sitting room. She returned to the kitchen. "Where did everything go?"

Jamie's lips curled into a grin, sparking a twinkle in his eyes. "Eli and I might have gotten a little carried away last night. We packed everything in the moving truck while you were asleep." He held his hands out, palms up, shoulders hunched. "It seemed like a good idea at the time."

"Please tell me you didn't unload everything into the new house."

"Of course not. Aunt Jackie wouldn't allow it."

"Then where's my stuff?"

"In the moving truck at the bungalow with Eli." He plopped down on a bar stool and pulled her down next to him. "Think about it, Mom. With New Year's on the horizon, we're in for another busy week at the market next week. We have to be out of here by Wednesday. If we get everything moved this weekend, we'll have time to clean this house after work on Monday and Tuesday and have it ready for the new owners by Wednesday. Today is a day of celebration, but tomorrow, after we exchange our gifts in the morning, we can spend the afternoon getting settled."

Sam let out a deep breath. "I guess that makes sense." She took a sip of her coffee. "I'm sorry, son. I haven't been able to wrap my mind around this move. I know I haven't been much help. I'm usually so organized."

"You've had a lot on your plate at work. And I didn't help any by dragging SoDiva into the mix."

Sam's face flushed pink. "How did you know I called her SoDiva?"

"I overheard you say it to Eli. A very clever and appropriate nickname if you ask me." Jamie reached across the counter for the bag of Krispy Kreme mini crullers. He opened the bag and stuffed two in his mouth before offering the bag to his mother.

Sam removed a doughnut and dunked it in her coffee. "I've been so distracted. No telling what I've forgotten. I guess it doesn't matter now. Ready or not, wedding chapel here we come."

❄

"Music! I forgot to organize any music for the ceremony," Sam said to Jamie as they ducked into the chapel out of the heavy falling snow.

In the absence of a dressing room for the bride, when she'd discussed the logistics of the ceremony with Pastor Paul, they decided she and Jamie would enter the church and walk down the aisle.

Jamie held his arm out to her and they moved to the double doorway leading to the small sanctuary. "We can sing Christmas carols," Jamie whispered.

She sent an elbow to his ribs. "I'm serious, Jamie. Eli is going to kill me. We can't get married without music."

"No, he's not, and yes, you can."

Pastor Paul saw them and gave a slight nod to a harpist who began playing "Canon in D."

She gripped her son's arm tighter and he smiled down at her. "See. Aunt Jackie hasn't forgotten a thing."

Annie appeared at her side, placing a small bouquet of white roses and Christmas greenery in her hands. As she glided down the aisle on her son's arm, Sam fixated on the altar, which was adorned with white poinsettias and huge bows of magnolia. Her breath caught at the sight of her handsome groom in his new gray suit that matched his smoky eyes. Standing next to him, looking like a princess in a white velvet dress with her dark hair curled in spirals and a bouquet of pink sweetheart roses in her hand, was her niece. What a great idea to have Bitsy be her flower girl. When she spotted Jackie in the first pew, she mouthed the words *thank you*.

Jamie kissed her on the cheek and handed her over to Eli. When they stepped up to the altar together, Sam shifted so she could see her family and loved ones behind them—only sixteen in number but taking up most of the pews in the small sanctuary. She smiled at her mother, who winked back at her.

Pastor Paul talked for a moment about his relationship with Sam before moving on to the ceremony. Surrounded by the people she loved most in the world, while the snow blanketed the frozen creek, Sam recited her marriage vows to her groom. Pastor Paul announced them husband and wife, they kissed amongst cheers from the congregation, and the harpist played Handel's "Allegro Maestoso" as they walked down the aisle, pausing to greet their family and friends along the way.

Sam stopped in her tracks when they reached the front steps of the church. There, idling at the curb, was her Jeep with red, white, and green Christmas lights wound around the rack on top.

Eli held out his hand. "Your chariot awaits, Mrs. Marshall."

"What is my car doing here? It was in my driveway thirty minutes ago when Jamie and I left to come here in his truck."

"Actually, it wasn't. I confiscated it last night. The original plan was to use my cruiser as the getaway car. Annie and Jamie were collaborating on the decorations. But, since cruisers don't do well in the snow, we had to get creative."

Placing her hands on his cheeks, she pulled his lips to hers. "Someone could've stolen my car. I was in such a hurry to get to the chapel to marry you, I didn't even notice it missing."

He took her by the hand and they rushed down the sidewalk to her Jeep. Eli took the long way to the bungalow, allowing them a few extra minutes to collect themselves. As they passed the market, Sam noticed a boxwood wreath with a white bow and silver bells hanging on the front door.

"More evidence of Jackie," she said, and he nodded. "She didn't miss a thing."

They were the last to arrive at the reception. Eli lifted Sam out of the Jeep and carried her up the shoveled front stairs and over the threshold of their new home.

Heidi and Annie were waiting for them inside. Heidi handed them silver goblets tied with white ribbons and filled with sparkling nonalcoholic wine. "Welcome home!" Annie said and Heidi added, "Best wishes for a long and happy life together."

"Hear, hear!" Jamie said and everyone lifted their glasses in a toast.

"Aunt Sam, you're here." Bitsy rushed into her arms, nearly knocking her off her feet.

Sam kissed the top of her head. "Hey there, kiddo. Having you waiting for me on the altar was the nicest surprise."

The little girl circled her. "You look beautiful, like a fairy princess." She wrinkled her nose. "All except the boots."

"It's snowing outside, silly. What else was I supposed to wear? I can't walk in the snow in my heels. And you're the one who looks like a princess. You stole the show." Sam knelt down beside her. "Tell me, are you excited about Santa Claus?"

She bobbed her head, her curls dancing around her shoulders. "I asked him to bring me a puppy. Something small and white and furry. Do you think it'll get lost in the snow when I take it outside to pee?"

This was the first Sam had heard mention of a puppy. "That's a good question, Bits." She twirled one of the girl's curls around her finger. "Maybe you should spread out some newspaper and let it do its business in the kitchen just in case."

"Speaking of kitchens . . ." Heidi held her hand out to Bitsy. "I have some cookies that need decorating, and I could really use your help."

Bitsy took her hand and skipped off beside Heidi on the way to the kitchen.

Sam caught sight of the Christmas tree—a ginormous Fraser fir in the center of the room decked out with thousands of twinkling white lights, white shell ornaments, and sheer silver ribbon. "This place looks amazing. That has to be the biggest Christmas tree I've ever seen." She roamed about the room inspecting the decor. Pillar candles in cylinder vases and magnolia garlands coated with a thin layer of silver metallic paint bedecked both mantels. Set for sixteen, the dinner table—covered in crisp white linens with a collection of mercury glass Christmas trees and elegant white flowers arranged in silver mint julep cups—ran parallel to the bank of windows, looking out on the snowy afternoon.

Heidi and her hired helper offered trays of canapés and refills of champagne while Sam and Eli spoke to each of their guests in turn. The room crackled with excitement for the wedding, the snow, and Christmas. Sam excused herself to powder her nose giving Eli a few minutes alone with his brother, Kyle, and sister-in-law, Shay. Upon her return, she sought out her sister who was warming her hands by the fire.

"I can't thank you enough for everything you've done for me," she said as she embraced Jackie. "Everything is simply perfect. How did you know I'd forget the music?"

"Experience has taught me there are five key ingredients to throwing a successful party. Venue, food, flowers, music, and booze," she said, ticking off each one on her fingers as she spoke. "In your case the booze means nonalcoholic sparkling wine."

Sam smiled. "Who needs alcohol when I have Eli? I want you to know I appreciate your efforts. I would never have been able to accomplish all this on my own."

Jackie pinched Sam's cheek. "You provided the venues. Both of them excellent choices, I might add. And we took care of the rest."

Sam eyed a pair of contemporary sofas upholstered in a soft hue of gray velvet. "Whose are those?"

"Yours, if you want them," Jackie said. "I ordered them for a client, but they don't fit her space. I can sell them to you at cost if you're interested. The style is what I had in mind when I first saw this place, but it might be too mod for your taste. I can always find somewhere to use them."

Sam lowered herself to one of the sofas and ran her fingers across the plush fabric. "They're different from anything I've ever owned, but I think they're the right choice for this room." She studied the Oriental rug at her feet. "Is the rug for sale as well? The colors are ideal."

Jackie left the fire and sat down next to Sam on the sofa. "The rug is an antique Tabriz and it belongs to me. I'm planning to use it in the house in Charleston, but I can find one similar for you if you like it."

"I can't afford an antique Oriental, Jackie."

"Then we'll buy a new one for half the price."

Faith appeared in front of them. "There you are. I've been looking all over for you." She wedged herself between her two sisters on the sofa. She kissed Sam's cheek. "You look stunning, and the ceremony was lovely."

"I was tickled to see Bitsy on the altar. She stole the show. But then she always does." Sam leaned in close to Faith. "I haven't heard you mention a puppy. I hope Santa doesn't disappoint her."

"Are you kidding me? Mike has spent the last three months researching breeds. He finally decided on a miniature cockapoo. He picked it up from Charleston late yesterday afternoon. One of the doctors from the hospital is keeping it for us until after the party tonight."

Warmth radiated through Sam's body. "I wish I could be there to see her face. She's going to be thrilled."

"By the way, I might have been wrong about your caterer. Heidi is channeling Bitsy's energy into decorating Christmas cookies. I just checked on her. I've never seen her so intent on a project before."

"Heidi is harmless, at least as far as I can tell." Sam

gestured at Annie and Cooper who were standing alone by the windows looking out at the snow. "Looks to me like we should worry more about Annie's infatuation with Cooper." Sam had not seen Annie and Cooper together in nearly a week, but she could tell something had shifted in their relationship. Their touches lingered. Their eyes smoldered. Their innocent flirtation had transitioned into unbridled young passion. "Have you talked to her about the birds and the bees yet?"

"Mike and I have both told her that she can talk to us about anything," Faith said.

"Please," Jackie huffed. "Annie is sixteen and Cooper is seventeen. I'm sure they know where babies come from."

Sam said, "Of course they know the facts, Jackie. I want to make sure Annie protects herself. I just hope she feels comfortable coming to one of us when it's time to see a doctor."

Sam kept one eye on Annie for the duration of the reception, throughout the four-course meal—soup, salad, and main course, with wedding cake for dessert—and afterward when everyone gathered around Sam and Eli while they opened their few gifts. Annie seemed ecstatic, bouncing about amongst the guests, but her mood shifted suddenly, and drastically, a short time later when they were cleaning up.

Most of the family had scattered. Jackie and Bill had left to get ready for the next event of the day—the family's annual Christmas Eve party at the farm. Mike and Faith had taken Bitsy home for a nap. Cooper and Sean were helping Eli and Jamie unload the moving truck. And Sam and Annie were clearing the table with Heidi. Annie disappeared into the kitchen with an armful of dirty plates and a smile on her face.

Several minutes later she returned with a haunted look on her face like she'd seen her father's ghost.

"Annie, honey, what happened?" Sam dropped her armload of soiled linens on the table and took Annie by the arm. "Did somebody say something to hurt your feelings?"

"I'm fine." Annie wrenched her arm free and moved to the fireplace.

Sam followed her. "Something is clearly wrong. Did you and Cooper have a fight?"

Annie inhaled an unsteady breath. "I accidentally knocked Heidi's purse off the chair in the kitchen and everything spilled out on the floor. When I knelt down to pick up her stuff, I saw her driver's license." Turning her back on Sam, Annie placed her forehead on the mantel. "Her name isn't Heidi Butler. Her real name is Sandra Bethune."

Sam gasped. "You mean—"

"Yes!" Annie said, her forehead still pressed to the mantel. "That's exactly what I mean. Heidi is my mother."

Luncheon Menu for Sam's Wedding Reception

Fried Oysters on Crackers
Smoked Salmon Bites with cucumber and cream cheese

Mini Spicy Crab Cakes with Lemon Aioli

She Crab Soup with Sherry

Pear and Arugula Salad
bosc pear, goat cheese, candied pecan, lemon vinaigrette

Shrimp and Grits
bacon, smoked sausage, green onions, mushrooms, garlic cheese grits

Ginger Spice Wedding Cake
real maple frosting and vanilla bean icing

A Note to Readers

Everything I've learned during my writing journey came together for me in *Her Sister's Shoes*. After exploring the brother/sister bond in *Saving Ben*, a study of three middle-aged sisters was a nice change of pace. I was thrilled, and pleasantly surprised, when *Her Sister's Shoes* began to fly of the e-bookshelves at Amazon, Barnes and Noble, and iTunes. I was even more excited when I began receiving wonderful emails from you, my faithful readers, sharing what you enjoyed about the novel and which sister you identified with the most. You saw the Sweeney sisters as I hoped you might—flawed women facing real-life issues as they struggle to balance career and home. I returned briefly to the brother/sister bond in *Merry Mary* and *Breaking the Story*, with Scottie Darden, an impulsive photojournalist whose brother, Will, saves her from herself when she gets into trouble. Which she often does. I'm not finished with Scottie and Will, but for the time being, my heart is deep in the Lowcountry with the Sweeney family.

While I love Richmond, Virginia, my home for the past twenty years, I miss the easy-going ways of the folks who reside in the Lowcountry. Writing about these quirky characters and their unique way of life is the next best thing to experiencing them on a daily basis. I love the beauty of the area—the marshlands and moss-draped trees—and the southern accents and local cuisine. I have become so immersed in the lives of these three special ladies that I dream about them at night, think about them during the day, and plot ways for them to keep you entertained.

I love hearing from you. Feel free to shoot me an email at ashleyhfarley@gmail.com or stop by my website at ashleyfarley.net for more information about my characters and upcoming releases. For a limited time, I'm offering a free e-story, *Heading Home,* for those who sign up for my newsletter. *Heading Home* offers an inside glimpse into Heidi's life. Click HERE to get your free copy. Your newsletter subscription will also grant you exclusive content, sneak previews, and special giveaways.

Acknowledgments

I AM BLESSED to have so many supportive people in my life, my friends and family who offer the encouragement I need to continue the pursuit of my writing career. On the top of my list, I would like to thank my husband, Ted, not only for believing in me, but for being my biggest fan and never letting me give up. I am forever indebted to my beta readers—Mamie Farley, Alison Fauls, and Cheryl Fockler—for the valuable constructive feedback, helping me with cover design, and promoting my work. I wouldn't survive a day in the world of publishing without my trusted editor, Patricia Peters, who challenges me to dig deeper and helps me to make my work stronger without changing my voice.

A special thanks to Damon Freeman and his crew at Damonza.com for their creativity in designing stunning covers and interiors, and for their patience in dealing with my fickleness and occasional temper tantrums.

Thank you to my family and friends for your continued support. I'm so very grateful to each and every one of you.

Thanks to Karen Stephens for answering my endless questions regarding real estate. Most importantly, to my children, Cameron and Ned, who provide inspiration for me every single day.

65636565R00102

Made in the USA
San Bernardino, CA
04 January 2018

'TIS THE SEASON FOR CHAOS.

Wedding bells will soon be ringing in the Lowcountry. All Sam Sweeney wants is to marry her man on Christmas Eve surrounded by family and friends. But emerging complications, some humorous and some not so humorous, threaten to converge and derail the best-laid plans during the busy stretch between Thanksgiving and Christmas.

Amidst the chaos—dealing with real estate, planning a wedding, running a seafood market, honoring traditions, and contending with teenagers—even the weather rears its head when the weatherman forecasts a white Christmas. Never has family support been more needed, but will it be enough to restore order and save the day?

Escape to the Lowcountry this Christmas where romance, intrigue, and holiday merrymaking await you.

ISBN 9780986167287

9 780986 167287